The Make-Believe Wives

The Make-Believe Wives

Darliss Batchelor

Word in Due Season Publishing, LLC

The Make-Believe Wives

Darliss Batchelor

Copyright © 2017 by Darliss Batchelor
All rights reserved

Word in Due Season Publishing, LLC
P.O. Box 210013
Auburn Hills, Michigan 48321-0921

Cover Design by Cover Me Book Covers

ISBN 13: 978-0-9829686-9-7

Library of Congress Control Number: 2017907999

Printed in the United States of America

Acknowledgements

God is just awesome! I thank Him for gifting me to tell stories and aligning my life such that I can walk in it with ease. I pray my work pleases You.

I must acknowledge my husband, Greg, for allowing me the grace to focus on my writing dreams. I love and respect you for being who you are.

I want to thank the editor for this project, Felecia Murrell. You pushed me as a writer and the book is better for it. I look forward to working together again.

Renee Luke of Cover Me Book Covers, you are a lifesaver and a talented and gifted cover designer. Thank you for everything!

I thank James Esnault, LeTeisha Lucas and LaToya Murchison of Creative Expressions Literary Services for serving as beta readers. I appreciate the time each of you took to read the manuscript and provide invaluable insight.

A special acknowledgement to my friend, Stacey Johnson for your willingness to provide much-needed information on police procedure. Thank you for your help.

Last, but not least, I must acknowledge every literary supporter regardless of your contribution to my writing journey. Whether you read one of my books, offered a word of encouragement or recommended my books to others, I appreciate you.

Chapter 1

Janay slammed the glass into the bottom of the sink and watched it break into a million pieces. She chased it with two plates and a bowl that were within reach. No need to worry about washing those. Frightened by the noise, her baby girl screamed and she joined her. Unlike Naomi, Janay's scream was from sheer frustration. She pulled herself together and went to gather her daughter from the adjoining family room. Naomi raised her arms as her mother approached and Janay picked her up. Once comforted, the toddler wiggled to get back to her playtime. Janay returned her to the center of the toys she had spread out over the family room floor and exhaled.

Her husband, Evan, had taken Nahla and Nia out for a daddy-daughter day. Naomi was too young for today's activity. Janay returned to the kitchen and stared at the glass and ceramic gumbo in the sink. She picked up a few of the larger pieces of glass and sat them on the granite countertop, mentally adding resealing it to her already overloaded to-do list. She remembered literally vibrating with excitement when they bought this stone. Now, it brought tears.

Janay went to the bathroom to wash her face, hoping it would make her feel better. She pulled the plush fire engine red face towel from the bar and ran cold water over it. Looking in the mirror, she noticed the frustration etched in her face and the tent city that had formed below her eyes. These had become her constant companions. She patted the area with the cold towel and went back to the family room to check on Naomi. Her routine had gotten old.

***

Janay watched as Evan moved bowls and plates around in the cabinet, undoubtedly looking for something in particular. Next, he searched the dishwasher. "Hmph," Evan said as he closed the door, looking at her with both hands on his waist, which usually meant he was stumped about something.

"Babe, do you know what happened to that blue bowl? I can't find it."

"Which one?" Janay asked trying to figure out the best way to tell him about his favorite cereal bowl's fate.

"We only had one. It was deep blue."

"It got broken. Accidentally. The other day," she replied.

Evan stepped down into the room and sat next to his wife on the beige leather sofa. "Is everything okay?"

"Yes. Why?"

"A lot of dishes are getting broken lately. I wonder why." He looked at her so intently it was clear he already knew the answer.

"You think so?" She tilted her head to the side.

"I keep finding broken dishes in the garbage. What's going on?" Evan reached for her hand.

"I drop a dish or two from time to time. The ceramic floor is unforgiving." She shrugged, "No big deal."

"If it was more than that you would tell me, right?"

"Yes, you would be the first to know."

Chapter 2

Evan had noticed a change in Janay a few months prior. She appeared unhappy. All of those broken dishes she brushed off as being accidentally destroyed was another indication something was wrong. He didn't know who she thought she was fooling. He knew she was intentionally breaking dishes. And though her reasons were unclear, he was sure the dishes weren't just jumping to their own demise.

He was sure she loved him and their daughters. But it seemed as though something was missing for her, as if she resented doing the things necessary to take care of the house and their family. The laundry went undone. The bathrooms weren't clean. The poor dishwasher was taking a beating every time she had to load it. Cabinet doors, as well as pots and pans, were slammed when she prepared food. When he tried to watch recordings of his favorite TV shows, Janay made her unhappiness known about that as well, sighing and grunting until she got his attention. When Evan asked her what was wrong, she simply said, "Nothing."

From time to time she seemed extremely frustrated when things required a little more effort than she wanted to expend.

Evan understood the concept but didn't know what to do to alleviate the problem.

He often wondered if they should elicit some sort of help around their 3,000 square foot Troy, Michigan home. He wasn't fond of the idea because that would mean strangers running through their home unsupervised. The home's five bedrooms, three and a half baths and basement man cave couldn't take too much time and effort to keep clean. The girls needed to learn how to manage their spaces as well. Eventually, they would share some of the household responsibilities giving Janay some much needed help. But, that wouldn't be for a while and he believed this was probably Janay's issue.

As her husband, he felt it was his job to fix the problem. How to fix it was another issue. What would make Janay happy? As he questioned himself regarding what to do to appease her, an idea presented itself. Perhaps, a change of scenery might help. The entire family could participate which would alleviate the need for a babysitter. She could get away from the house and her job for a weekend or so, which could help as well. Evan knew exactly what to do.

Chapter 3

"Janay," Evan yelled while she prepared dinner for the family. Nahla and Nia were taking turns reading to Naomi. While they were entertaining their baby sister, in reality it was reading practice for the two of them.

Evan came into the kitchen. Janay could see the excitement on his face. "Come outside for a minute. I got something I want you to see."

She looked down at her red t-shirt and gray sweatpants covered with flour. "I can't go outside looking like this."

Evan's eyes roamed her body from head to toe. "You're okay. We're just going to the driveway."

Janay stepped onto the porch. A travel trailer was connected to her father-in-law's Chevrolet Suburban. "What's that?" She asked pointing at the vehicles.

"Come look inside." Evan stepped into the trailer and extended his hand to help her inside. It looked like a mini-home. A kitchenette complete with a sink, stainless steel refrigerator and stove surrounded by chocolate brown cabinets met them upon entering. On one end of the trailer was a set of cocoa recliners and a matching couch. The opposite end held a living space with a fireplace, leather couch and dining set. A bedroom and bathroom completed the interior of the home on wheels.

"This is very nice. Are you trying to tell me you're going on a trip with the guys or something?"

"Not exactly." Evan pulled her close. "I've noticed you're not your usual self and I want you to be happy. I thought if we did something fun as a family, like a camping trip, it might help."

Janay's shoulders slumped. Tears filled her eyes as she pulled away from Evan, "No, thank you. Being outdoors is your thing, not mine. You know I don't like bugs and the woods are full of them."

"Honey, I'm trying to make you happy. You seem so sad and I don't know what to do about it. Please help me understand what's going on. I don't like being in the dark."

"I give you credit for noticing there was a problem and trying to eliminate it, Evan. But, the problem is much deeper than a camping trip could ever resolve."

Evan's mouth hung open as he watched his wife walk out of the trailer and up the driveway into the house without another word. It seemed instead of helping, he'd upset her more. He decided to back away for a while and keep an eye on things. All he could do was hope things got better.

Chapter 4

Janay found Evan in the home office and began speaking before she could change her mind. "Can you come into the family room? I need to talk to you."

"Give me a few minutes. I'll be right there." Evan glanced at his wife and then back at his laptop, shutting it down.

Minutes later, he settled onto the couch next to her. Hoping to create a relaxing environment, Janay offered Evan a croissant from the collection on the table in front of them as smooth jazz flowed through the room.

"What's up?" Evan wondered aloud, looking over the preparations.

"What I'm getting ready to say doesn't have anything to do with you or our marriage. This is about me."

"Now, you've got me worried."

Janay sipped from her cup and took a bite of her croissant. After a long pause, she continued, "Being a wife and mother has been the whole of my adult life."

"I know all the history, Janay. Remember, I was there." Evan nervously laughed.

"I haven't been at peace for months and didn't know why. I feel overwhelmed, exhausted, like I'm on the verge of a breakdown. I need to make a change."

"What kind of change are you talking about?"

She took a deep breath and released it. "I think I need to go away for a while."

"Go away where?"

"I'm not exactly sure where. But, I feel like I just need to rest, rejuvenate, experience some things, and find myself."

"I'm so confused. At first you were talking about being tired. Now, you're talking about needing to find yourself. What is really going on?"

"I missed out on a lot getting married so young, Evan. I never had a chance to grow into myself. You know what I mean?"

"No, I don't," Evan shook his head.

"Do you know you're the only guy I ever dated? I never went to a school dance or even to the mall to shop with my friends. Actually, I never even really had friends."

"That was a long time ago. What does that have to do with today?"

"I want to experience life on my own for a while."

Evan placed his head in his hands then ran them through his hair. "What? You want to... you cannot be serious. Am I being punked?"

"I've been thinking about this for a while. It's what I need to do for myself."

"Janay, I don't even know how you could think this is a good idea. What are the girls and I supposed to do?"

"That's part of the problem. Everything is always about you and the kids. Why can't it be about me for once?"

"When you're a wife and mother, it's supposed to be about us. Not just you."

"You don't care about my needs as long as you're getting yours met. Is that what you're saying?"

"I do care about your needs and your feelings. But, you can't just expect me to help you pack your bags. We need you."

"I desperately need this break, but I wouldn't feel right about leaving without your agreement."

"In that case, I guess you won't be going," Evan stood and faced his wife. "Is there anything else you want to discuss?"

"I guess the king has spoken, huh?"

"I guess he has," Evan said as he left the room.

Chapter 5

"The obstacle course competition will begin in fifteen minutes. Get your teams together and meet at the playground," the events coordinator at Evan's family reunion announced.

"Mommy, Daddy, come on, let's go," Nahla said as she tugged on Evan and Janay.

"Honey, I don't think we're going to participate. I don't think Mommy wants to," Evan replied.

"You don't want to?" Nahla turned to her mom, stomping her feet and poking her lips out. We always do the obstacle course."

"Of course we're going to do it." Janay reached over and hugged her daughter. "Go get Nia and Aunt Cherlynn. We'll meet you at the playground."

Nahla ran off in search of her sister and aunt.

Janay turned to her husband, "Why would you tell her that?"

Evan shrugged. "I thought you didn't want to do anything with us,"

"That's not true. So, chill on the attitude please," Janay said, frowning.

"I don't know how to do that. I've been thinking about this and I'm wondering what this is really about."

"What do you think it's about?" Janay stopped walking and faced Evan.

Evan folded his arms and leaned against a tree, "I don't know. Do you want a divorce?"

"No, I don't. I want a break in the action to help me be a more fulfilled person. I thought you understood that."

"It's hard not to think there's something else going on when this came out of the blue."

"There is nothing else going on, Evan."

"If you say so."

"We'd better get over to the race before Nahla comes back."

***

After the race, the women took the children to the waterpark and the men played dominos. Evan decided to use the time to think. He sat at a picnic table situated under a huge tree away from the group. Just when his thoughts took him away from reality, his father sat next to him and handed him a cold beverage. Father and son sat silently for a few minutes.

"Son, is everything okay?"

"Yeah. Everything's good." Evan responded dryly.

Evan's father nodded. "Things good with Janay and the girls, too?"

"Yep, just great," Evan lifted his beverage to his mouth.

"Do you want to talk about it?"

"Pop, I don't think I'm ready to discuss what's going on," Evan stared into the distance.

"I respect that. If you don't mind, I'll just sit here with you a while longer."

"Alright."

After a few moments, Evan broke the silence.

"Have you and Mom ever thought about splitting up?"

"It never crossed my mind, but you'll have to ask your mother if she thought about it."

"That's good to know."

"Are you ready to talk now?" He asked looking at his son.

"I don't know if this is the right place for that."

"Follow me." Evan's father rose and walked to the parking lot with Evan following. The two men got into his dad's 1976 Corvette and pulled out of the parking area. They rounded the park until they arrived at the lake and stopped. The two could talk privately here even with the T-tops out.

"Alright. Tell me what's going on."

"Janay says she needs to go find herself. I thought everything was good between us until she made this announcement."

"I see. The infamous lost self. I thought this might happen."

"How did you know? Did Janay say something to Mom about this?"

"Not that I know of, son. I didn't think she was ready for the type of relationship you wanted. She wasn't as mature as you and she lived a sheltered life. I thought she might realize that someday."

"That's what Janay said. Why didn't you tell me?"

"I tried to but you wouldn't listen. You were in love and couldn't wait to get married."

"I thought you were hoping we would break up."

Evan's father chuckled. "Even if we were against you and Janay getting married, we never would've given you bad advice to break you up. Now, let me tell you something else."

"I'm listening."

"You can't make that woman stay with you no more than we could make you wait to get married," Pop said with a pointed finger.

"So, I should just let her go?"

"I'm saying you can't stop her. Prepare yourself for the possibility."

Chapter 6

Janay felt a presence at her desk. She looked up and found the piercing eyes of Frank Scott, a contract employee, peering at her over the top of her cubicle. Frank had been around for about eight months working on a new computer system installation project. She knew the computer industry tended to attract unusual individuals, but this guy seemed to be in a class all by himself.

"Hey, Frank," she said, "What can I do for you?"

"What are you doing for lunch today?"

"I haven't decided yet. Are you going out?"

Frank nervously looked around the office. "Yeah, it looks like everyone else has already gone to The Tavern."

"Oh. I must have missed the email on the group lunch thing." Janay looked around at the empty office space.

"So, are you coming? We can walk over together."

"Maybe, I will. Let me run to the ladies' room and I'll meet you at the elevator in a few minutes."

***

Frank and Janay stepped inside The Tavern. The dark wood décor and stained glass windows provided an old-world backdrop for the Italian restaurant. The bar area was to the right of the lobby and hosted ample counter space and accompanying stools. The edges of the area held high top tables suited for small parties of four or less.

Janay stood at the entrance to the main dining room. "Where is everyone? I don't see anyone from the office here," she wondered aloud, looking around for familiar faces.

"I don't know. Maybe I got the wrong restaurant."

Janay wasn't comfortable having lunch alone with Frank. They had gone to lunch and participated in other activities many times with the group but never just the two of them.

"Maybe we should go back to the office. I should probably be eating what I brought for lunch anyway."

"We might as well eat since we're here." Frank took her hand and swung it back and forth a couple of times.

Janay looked down at their intertwined fingers and wondered what was going on.

She gently removed her hand from his, "Well...okay, I have a taste for their Italian Macaroni and Cheese anyway."

The two were seated at a table in the middle of the large dining room. Frank whispered something to the hostess who moved them to a booth in the corner that was much too cozy for a lunch between coworkers. The waiter came by shortly after and took their order.

"Why do I feel this was all a setup?" Janay asked.

Frank chuckled. "What makes you think that?"

"Everyone in the office knew about the lunch plans except me, no one from the office is here and now we've moved from the table to a private booth. I'm wondering why you arranged this."

Frank shifted in his seat. It was obvious he was uncomfortable. He glanced at Janay a couple of times and then looked down at the table for a few minutes.

"How are things at home with Evan?"

"Why are you asking?"

"I've noticed whenever Evan's name comes up, your whole demeanor changes. A woman like you should never be unhappy." Frank's assessment was dead-on, but Janay wouldn't admit it.

"I never said I was unhappy."

"You didn't have to. I can see it." Once again, Frank shifted in his seat and appeared to be deep in thought. "Do you think people marry the wrong person sometimes?"

"I suppose so."

"What if you discovered you married the wrong man? What would you do?"

Now it was Janay's turn to fidget. "I think we should change the subject."

"Do you think people should stay with their spouse even if they're unhappy or should they find the one God created just for them?"

"Maybe we should get our meals to go," she said looking for their waitress.

"No worries. Relax. I'm just making conversation, trying to get to know you a little better."

This whole scenario didn't feel right. Janay pondered what could be going on in Frank's mind as he took her hands in his to bless their food when it was placed before them.

Chapter 7

The spring breeze from the open window in Evan and Janay's master bedroom flowed over their bodies like a caress. The soft white sheer curtains danced in the wind as the couple's lovemaking came to an end. Their legs and bodies remained intertwined as they embraced one another.

Evan felt reassured he and Janay would be okay and that Janay would get whatever she felt she was missing without leaving this place of love, tranquility and peace. Evan knew he could not, would not allow this woman to leave him, even temporarily. If she did, it would be like breath leaving his body. He wouldn't survive it. He didn't understand what Janay was thinking or feeling. He just knew he couldn't allow those things to keep them from experiencing moments like this.

"What are you thinking about?" Evan asked his wife.

"I'm just laying here enjoying the moment."

"I'm thinking about what you told me the other day. I had no idea there was an issue."

"Maybe I should've talked to you before it got to this point."

"Yes, you should have."

"It took me a while to figure it all out."

"Why don't I send you on a personal vacation? You can go wherever you want."

"Evan, I know you're trying to fix this. But, you can't. I can never get back that time."

"Leaving won't change that."

"That's a good point." After a few moments of silence, Janay said, "I made up my mind and this is what I want to do."

"Is there someone else?"

"What makes you think there's someone else?"

"Because that's the only thing that would make sense."

"Evan, I don't want anyone but you. Please believe me."

Evan went silent. She took his chin in her hand and turned his head toward hers, meeting his eyes. "I love you. No other man could ever come between us."

Chapter 8

Janay sat at her desk and checked the current day's to-do list, crossing off the tasks she had completed and moving the unfinished tasks to the next day's list. That done, she reviewed her calendar to see if she had any meetings she needed to prepare for. As she packed her belongings in her work bag, Frank came to her desk.

"Are you ready to walk out?" Frank asked.

"I'm ready to do just that. I've got to pick up the girls tonight." Janay left her workspace and headed toward the elevator with Frank following closely behind her.

"What happens if you don't pick them up?"

"If I can't get them for some reason, I can call Evan or my sister to pick them up."

"So, they won't be abandoned or anything like that?"

Janay glanced at Frank over her shoulder. "No. Why are you asking all of these questions about my daughters?"

"I was just wondering," Frank said as they got off the elevator and proceeded through the lobby. "Where did you park?"

"I got here a little late this morning so I parked in the public lot a couple blocks away."

"I don't want you walking over there by yourself. Let me drive you over to your car. That way I'll know you're safe."

"That's really not necessary, Frank. Thanks anyway." Janay didn't want to be alone with Frank again.

"No, I insist. I'm parked in the employee lot across the street. Come on. I'll take you over there."

"I don't want to inconvenience you."

"Janay, it's no problem. I've got to go to my car anyway and I'll pass right by the lot you're parked in."

"Okay, since you insist."

"I'll feel better that way. I'm parked right over here."

***

"Do you think I'm attractive?" Frank asked as he pulled his car onto the street.

Janay looked straight ahead. "I really don't look at you like that."

"I think you do. I've seen you looking at me."

"Frank, I don't know what you think you saw but you're mistaken."

"Nope, I've seen you admiring my physique."

I don't know where this is going but..."

"I want to have mind sex."

"Mind sex? You have lost your mind." Janay surveyed the surrounding area trying to decide if she could jump out of the moving car without breaking a leg or some other body part. With the way Frank was talking, she was almost willing to take the chance.

"We can make love with our minds. We don't have to touch," he said turning his attention back to the road after briefly glancing at Janay. "Unless you want to."

Janay struggled to find the right response. Frank seemed emotionally unstable and she didn't want to upset him. Since she was in his car, she reasoned she had to play along until she could get out. On the other hand, she wanted to be clear he understood they weren't in some type of intimate relationship.

"Nothing can ever happen between us, Frank, mentally or physically."

Janay turned toward Frank, shocked to find him staring at her. The look in his eyes was frightening. *Dear Lord, how did I allow myself to get into this situation?*

"Just wait and see. I believe with all my heart that we're going to be together forever." He grabbed her hand and squeezed it.

"Um, Frank. You just passed the lot where my car is parked." *Oh, Lord! What have I gotten myself into? I have got to get out of this car right now.* It no longer mattered that the car was still moving. She pulled on the door handle. It was locked. Janay took a deep breath. *I'm just being overly paranoid. Besides, staying in the car and hoping for the best with Frank is probably a lot safer than being alone in this area.* She stared out the window as Frank drove further away from her vehicle.

"I know, my love," Frank said with a grin that made her stomach sink.

Janay didn't know what he had in mind, but she knew she was in trouble. *God, please help me.*

Chapter 9

It had been weeks since Janay made the announcement she wanted some time away but everything seemed to be back to normal. The children never even knew there was anything going on. Evan remained on guard because of his father's words. He decided if Janay didn't bring up the issue, neither would he. His prayer was that a momentary spike in estrogen or something had caused her unrest.

Evan stood in the kitchen and went through the mail. As he read over a letter, his phone rang. He saw it was the children's babysitter, Faith Richards, and wondered why she was calling.

"Hello."

"Hi, this is Faith."

"Is everything okay with the girls?" Evan inquired as he dropped the letter on the kitchen island.

"I'm calling because Janay hasn't picked up the girls yet and it isn't like her to be late."

"I'm sorry about that," Evan responded worriedly. "I don't know what's going on. She normally lets me know if she's held up. One of us will be there shortly to pick the girls up."

"Okay, but I'm going to have to charge a late pickup fee."

"I understand. I'm sure this is just an oversight on her part."

"I'm sure it is. The girls are a little hungry so I'm going to give them a snack. Hopefully, one of you will be here to pick them up by the time they're finished eating."

"We'll see you in a few." Evan hung up the phone. "Hmm, wonder what happened," he wondered aloud. It wasn't like Janay to forget their daughters. He called Janay's cell phone. It went straight to voicemail. He called Janay's boss to see if she was working late.

"Janay left quite some time ago. She said she had to pick up the girls."

"How long ago was that?"

"It's been well over an hour or so ago. Is something wrong?"

"The girls are still with the babysitter. I don't know where Janay is."

"Just let me know when you find her so I know she's safe. I'll keep my cell phone on so I can be reached. It doesn't matter what time it is, please call me."

"Thanks. I'll be sure to do that."

Evan considered calling his mother-in-law. He twirled his phone on the counter for a few minutes before finally picking it up and selecting her number from his contacts. He rubbed his head as the phone rang.

"Hello."

"Big Momma, how you doing?"

"I'm good."

"You sound good."

"Why, thank you, son. Is everything okay?"

"I'm looking for Janay, Big Momma. Have you seen her?"

"No, I haven't seen her in a few days."

"She didn't pick the girls up yet and I don't know where she is. Her boss said she left over an hour ago."

"She probably got held up at the grocery store or something. She'll show up."

"I hope so, Big Momma. Did Janay seem okay the last time you saw her?"

"I'm going to be honest with you, dear. She told me what's been going on. I don't know what's behind it, but I've been praying about this situation."

"Don't stop praying. We need it."

"I believe she's just going through a little something. It's all going to work out fine."

"I hope so, Big Momma. I guess I'd better pick up the girls so Faith can get on with her evening."

"Alright, honey. One of you call me when Janay gets in."

"Okay. We'll be in touch."

Chapter 10

"Nia, what's wrong?" Evan asked his middle child who was bawling in the middle of the night. It had been a month since Janay left and the family was still adjusting.

"My ears hurt and I'm hot," a shivering yet sweaty Nia responded.

"Hmmm. Both of your ears are hurting?"

"Yes, Daddy. Ow!" She howled as another wave of pain rushed through her ears.

"I'll be right back," Evan went in search of the thermometer.

"I'm going to take your temperature. Okay?"

"Okay."

Evan placed the thermometer against Nia's forehead and waited until it beeped. He looked at the digital readout.

"Oh, my goodness. You definitely have a fever." Evan deduced a visit to the emergency room was in order. This was where Janay usually excelled. She could mobilize the family even in the middle of the night. With three young children he'd seen her do it numerous times. However, she wasn't there so it was up to him. He didn't want to wake the other girls but he couldn't leave them home alone either. He stood there trying to determine his course of action. *I'll call Big Momma and ask her. She'll know what to do,* Evan thought as he reached for his phone.

"Oh, Lord. It's three am. Is it bad news about Janay?" Big Momma sounded as though she was wide-awake.

"No, Big Momma. It's Nia. I need to take her to get some medical attention, but I don't want to wake the other girls. I don't know how to make all of this happen."

"Is that all?" Big Momma chuckled. "Boy, you got me all worked up. I'm sure Cherlynn won't mind coming over there while you see about Nia."

"Thanks. I knew you would know what to do. I'll get Nia dressed."

***

Evan settled Nia and called the babysitter. "Good morning, Faith. This is Evan."

"Good morning. You're running a little late this morning. Is everything okay?"

"I just got back from the emergency room. Nia has an ear and sinus infection, which brings me to why I'm calling. I'm staying home with her today so I won't be bringing the girls this morning."

"Thank goodness it wasn't anything serious. I can come over there and take care of things. That way, you don't have to miss work."

"I couldn't ask you to do that. I'll pay you for today anyway since it's past your cancellation time."

"Evan, really. It wouldn't be an imposition and by the way, you didn't ask. I volunteered. I've done it before."

"I do need to go in, but I just wouldn't feel right about you coming all the way over here."

"I'm done discussing this. I'll be there in about a half hour."

"There is one condition though."

"What is it?"

"You have to let me pay extra since you're making a house call."

"If you must. I'll see you soon."

***

Evan pulled the car into the garage after getting off work and immediately felt the pang of loneliness that had been haunting him. Looking at his wife's car reminded him of her absence. The authorities found it almost immediately in a parking lot near her job. Unfortunately, they weren't as helpful in their efforts to find Janay. It seems, as an adult, she could leave whenever she wanted; go wherever she wanted for as long as she wanted without any warning or explanation. Since there was no sign of her being hurt or that she left against her will, the only thing Evan could do was file a missing person's report and hope she reappeared unharmed.

He sat for a minute thinking about all that had occurred. He couldn't believe Janay actually went through with the separation or whatever it was she wanted. Janay had always been devoted to their family so he couldn't understand what caused this shift in her attitude. He wondered if she was experiencing some sort of chemical imbalance. What he did know was that her absence shook the foundation of their family in a way he knew they wouldn't easily recover from.

He got out of his car and the unmistakable scent of food assaulted his nostrils. Could Janay be home? Evan rushed into the house toward the kitchen.

"Hi, Evan."

"Hey, Faith. It smells wonderful in here. What are you cooking?" Evan was disappointed.

"Just a little chicken gumbo. I hope you don't mind. I rambled through your fridge and cabinets trying to see what you had. Is that okay?"

Evan didn't know what to say. Just a few minutes ago he thought things had returned to normal. Now, he knew they hadn't. The emotional rollercoaster he was on took a dive and he couldn't stop the dam from breaking. Tears streamed down his cheeks. The sobs he'd fought so hard to control were now escaping from his throat. Unable to control his emotions, he released all of the sadness that had built up inside of him.

Faith ran to Evan's side unsure of how to respond to him. She had been the family's babysitter since Nahla was born. They had become friendlier as the years passed but embracing Evan didn't seem to fall within the bounds of their relationship. Yet, her heart broke as she watched this normally strong man crumble before her eyes. She wrapped her arms around him and allowed him to empty his soul onto her shoulder. Once he was empty, he stood and reached for some paper towel to clean his face.

"I'm sorry. I didn't mean to unload like that. It's been so difficult missing Janay and taking care of the girls. Please forgive me. That won't happen again."

"And, here I thought you just didn't like gumbo." The two broke out into a hearty laughter that lightened the mood.

Chapter 11

"Well, well, if it isn't my handsome son-in-law and my gorgeous granddaughters. Come on in here and let Big Momma see you," Janay's mother opened the door to her home.

Nahla, Nia and Naomi ran to their grandmother and she gathered all three into her arms. Big Momma released and examined them one by one. There was something different about them. She looked at Evan and realized there was something different about him, too. They looked well cared for.

"Look at these beautiful hair-dos," she commented regarding the girls' braided hairstyles. "Who did your hair?"

"Miss Faith did it. Am I pretty?" Nia asked.

"You're always beautiful. All of you are. Cherlynn, can you come here for a minute?"

"Yes, ma'am," Janay's sister said as she entered the dining area, "Hey, Evan. I didn't know you were here."

"Hey, sis-in-law." Evan embraced his sister-in-law. Cherlynn was older than Janay and lived with their mother, Big Momma, so neither had to live alone.

"Momma, did you need something?"

"Yes, would you mind taking the girls up the street to the ice cream shop? I need to talk to Evan."

"Girls, do you want to get some ice cream?" Cherlynn asked her nieces.

"Yay!" Nia yelled. Naomi mimicked her. Nahla remained silent, focusing on her father.

"Daddy, will you be okay if we go get ice cream?" Nahla asked.

"Sure, baby. I'll be fine. Go ahead with Aunt Cherlynn. Have fun."

As the group exited, Evan sat down at the kitchen table and Big Momma poured him a cup of coffee. She dressed it the way she knew he liked it and placed it before him.

"Evan. How are you, dear?"

"I'm as well as can be expected. How are you?"

"I'm doing good considering what's going on," Big Momma paused for a minute before continuing. "So, Faith has been helping out with the girls, huh?"

"Yeah, she's a godsend. I needed some help."

"You know we're here. We can help, too. You don't have to just depend on Faith."

"I know. "

"Not unless you're wanting to call on her all of the time," Big Momma said.

"It sounds like there's something else you're trying to say," Evan leaned his elbows on the table.

"I've just been noticing Faith stepping in quite a bit where the girls are concerned and it makes me wonder what she's doing for you."

"Are you asking me if Faith and I are in a relationship?"

"That's one way to put it. Are you?"

"I'm still married. I don't have room to get involved with anyone else like that."

"Well, you need to be careful because you're vulnerable and those girls are, too. You and Faith could easily end up in a relationship you didn't count on."

"Faith and I have a friendly business relationship. There's nothing more than that."

"Umm hmm."

Chapter 12

News blared from the TV in the family room as Evan sat on the couch. Though it appeared he was engrossed in what was on, his mind was really on his missing wife. He had hoped the TV would distract him from his thoughts.

His heart was breaking not only for himself, but also his daughters. They missed Janay terribly and he saw subtle signs of the pain they were in. Faith's presence helped in a multitude of ways. She made sure homework was done. She prepared healthy meals and insured they all had fun.

"Hey, Daddy," Nahla said as she entered the family room, breaking Evan's concentration.

"Hey, baby girl. You need something?"

"When is Mommy coming home?" Seven year-old Nahla inquired as she crawled onto her father's lap and laid her head on his chest.

"I don't know, Honey Bear. I'm sure she'll be home any day now."

"Did she go to find her happiness?"

"What do you mean by that?" Evan inquired.

"I heard her talking on the phone about looking for it."

"Hmm, I see."

"Were we bad, Daddy? Is that why she wasn't happy with us?"

"No, Honey Bear. This has nothing to do with you. You are the best daughters in the whole wide world."

"Well, if she left because we were bad, we can fix that. I'll be a good girl and I bet I can get Nia and Naomi to be good, too.

Then, maybe Mommy will come back. What do you think, Daddy?"

"I don't want you worrying about this. It will all work out. Why don't you get your sisters and we'll have popcorn and watch a movie."

"Can we watch one of my movies?"

"Yes, whatever movie you want to watch."

"Okay, Daddy. I just wish Mommy was here for movie night... maybe next time."

"Yes, Honey Bear. Maybe next time."

***

After putting the girls to bed, Evan sat in bed reading through the pile of newspapers that had grown since Janay left. Time for reading was slim as he adjusted to taking care of the family without her. Melancholy visited him when he came upon the wedding announcements. He looked over to Janay's side of their king size bed where she hadn't slept in weeks. He touched the wedding band he still wore and twisted it around his finger. The motion of going around and around in circles mirrored his thoughts.

His world had been turned upside down. He wondered if Janay decided to leave without his agreement even though she promised not to. He thought everything was good between them until she got the desire to "find herself." Then, without warning, she was gone.

Faith's presence in his life cushioned the fall somewhat. She took up the slack around the house and not just where the girls were concerned. The two of them watched movies together they deemed the girls too young to see. During their outings, she seemingly fit right into the empty space Janay left. Considering all of that, he now understood what his mother-in-law was saying. The relationship between him and Faith could be on the verge of becoming something different than originally intended.

He didn't think he was ready to move on relationally. He still hoped his wife would return and they could resolve her issues. However, it had been months since he'd seen or heard from her so he needed to accept the possibility he would have to live without her.

Faith was certainly a sweet person and an asset to him and his daughters. She genuinely cared about his children and was obviously willing to do whatever it took to see they didn't miss out on anything.

If Evan was honest with himself, he enjoyed her presence as well. He wondered if…. No, he couldn't allow himself to think about him and Faith getting together. Being the attractive, intriguing woman she was, she had to have numerous men interested in her. Faith hadn't mentioned anyone, but he was sure there had to be someone.

The truth was his feelings for her were indeed changing. When she wasn't around, he was trying to find a reason to see her. When they were together, he was content. It almost felt like love, but Evan reasoned it couldn't be anything more than deep like. Could it?

Chapter 13

"I haven't seen you in a while. Where have you been?"
Faith's friend Macie asked as they settled into their booth at their
favorite lunch spot.

"I've been around," Faith responded.

"No, you haven't. We used to hang out at least once a
week and I think the last time we did that was more than two
months ago."

"Excuse me," Faith said as she pulled a ringing cell phone
from her purse. "I have to take this." Faith shifted in her seat and
placed a hand over her ear so she could hear the caller better. "Hi,
this is Faith." She listened to the person on the other end as a
smile lit across her face. "That sounds like fun. What time?" Even
though the caller couldn't see her, she nodded in agreement.
"Alright, Evan. I'll see you then. Bye."

Macie grinned conspiratorially at her friend. "I think I know
what's been keeping you busy."

"What?"

"You got a new man. Why didn't you tell me? I thought I had
offended you."

"What man?"

"The one you just finished talking to. You know you've got to give me all the details," Macie leaned closer to hear about Faith's new friend.

"That was Evan."

"So I heard. Tell me about him."

"He's Nahla, Nia and Naomi's father. You know… the girls I babysit."

"Well, why is that married man calling you on the weekend and what is the fun you're getting into with him?"

"Since his wife left—"

Macie whispered, "His wife left? You didn't tell me that."

"He hasn't heard from her in weeks, so, I've been helping out. Tonight is fun night with the girls."

"Babysitters don't do fun nights."

"I love and care about the children," Faith said with her palms up.

"Faith, we've been friends for a long time and I think I know you pretty well. You don't get this attached to the families you work for."

"Well, this time I did."

"You're putting your life on hold so you can be a make-believe wife and mother for Evan and his children."

"That's not true."

"Have you given up on the Chocolate One?"

"I'm not sure I'm ready to give him the type of relationship he wants."

"It sounds like you're ready to give it to Evan."

"It's not like that. I'm just trying to help. "

"You need to help yourself and get on with your life. Evan can take care of himself and his daughters."

Chapter 14

Faith picked up her phone and called Evan. Before she realized she had, indeed, crossed the line from babysitter to something different, she had agreed to go out with him and the girls a few weeks ago. But, Macie was right. Her life was secondary to what was going on with the Ingrams and the only way to reverse that was to gradually stop participating in extracurricular activities. She would have to stick to basic caregiving duties only. As she waited for Evan to answer, she convinced herself once more it was the right thing to do. It would take time and it would hurt a little but it had to be done.

"Hey, Faith. Are you on your way?" Evan asked when he answered the phone.

"Um, not exactly. I don't think I'm going to make it."

"What's going on? This is the third time in the last week or two you couldn't hang out with us."

"Nothing's wrong. I just have some other things going on right now."

"I feel like there's something you're not saying," Evan responded.

"A friend of mine pointed out that I've been absent from my life."

"What does that mean?"

"It means I'm not doing much of anything that doesn't involve you and the kids, and I'm not sure that's healthy for me," Faith said.

"Someone said something similar to me too."

The two sat in silence for several moments pondering the meaning behind what others had observed.

"What are we doing, Evan?"

"I'm not sure."

"I think our feelings got ahead of us. We need to get them back in line."

"Or not."

***

The following morning, Evan, Faith and the girls slid into the church pew next to each other. A rumble rose from the congregation as they moved into the pews together. The various grunts, lip-smacking and glances between parishioners increased Faith's discomfort. Evan seemed oblivious to what was happening and appeared to be planning to sit next to her. She shook her head and sat the girls between them.

"The text for this morning's message is 'Is it love?'" intoned Pastor Willis. "Look at your neighbor and ask them that question."

Evan and Faith looked at each other and smiled in response. "This week's teaching is being taken from the thirteenth chapter of First Corinthians. This text is called the 'love chapter' as it helps us understand what love is and what it is not. The word love has almost become cliché. It no longer carries the weight it should. People are jumping in and out of relationships and calling it love, but most people don't know what love really looks like. People of God, sex does not equal love. God sent me here this morning to clear the concept of love up for someone. Let's look at the text."

"Amen," several people exclaimed.

As Pastor Willis expounded on the definition of love and how it should be expressed, Faith's thoughts swirled.

Can I be falling in love with this man? She stole a glance at Evan only to be met by his stare.

Like magnets, their hands edged along the back of the pew toward the other. Their fingers touched, and the electricity that passed between them surprised her. The expression on Evan's face said he felt it too. Though no words were spoken aloud, the silent communication was clear. The fire of romance had been lit and they both felt the flame.

Chapter 15

Evan pulled into Big Momma's driveway. He and his daughters exited the car. He needed to share some important news and he wasn't sure how she would take it, given the circumstances. Nevertheless, he wanted her to be aware.

Looking at his young daughters as they ran toward their grandmother's door, Evan rubbed his sweaty palms against his pants leg and swiped at the sheen of perspiration on his forehead. How would this affect them? They were his priority and he wanted to insure their emotional well-being. However, he'd made a decision and though he would be sensitive to everyone else's feelings, his needs also needed to be addressed.

The first step in the process was to tell Big Momma and hopefully get her support. Otherwise, her rejection could make it difficult and uncomfortable for everyone.

The girls knocked on the door and rang the doorbell. Cherlynn answered the door. The girls greeted their aunt with hugs and kisses then disappeared into the family room where Big Momma was napping while Cherlynn went to her room. The girls shook their grandmother until she woke up and grabbed them in her arms as she always did.

"Hey, y'all. What y'all doing here?" Big Momma asked.

"Do you have some time? I need to talk to you," Evan said, shifting his weight from one foot to the other.

Big Momma observed Evan's body language and said to her granddaughters, "Sure. Girls, go upstairs and see what Aunt Cherlynn is doing." The girls scampered up the stairs to spend time with their aunt.

After the girls left the room, she addressed her son-in-law once again. "Come on and sit down."

Evan sat on the edge of the loveseat next to Big Momma's recliner with his head lowered and his fingers interlaced.

"What's going on? Is it Janay?"

"No, it's not Janay. It's me. You were right about Faith and I. We developed some feelings for each other." Evan glanced at his mother-in-law. "I know you might not like this, but I felt you needed to know."

"It was bound to happen with the time you two spend together. Are you sure about your feelings?"

"Yes, I'm positive. She's become part of our family. If it weren't for her, I'm sure things would have fallen apart by now."

"You're going to have to do better than that. If that was all it took, you'd be in love with me and Cherlynn too." The two shared a chuckle.

"I'm struggling to stay faithful to a marriage that doesn't even exist. At the same time, it feels like I'm cheating on Janay. I want to move on and don't want to feel guilty about doing it."

"I think you need to settle things with Janay before you go starting another relationship."

"I would if I knew where she was."

"I know, son. Tell me. Have you prayed about this situation?"

"I've spent some time talking to God about it."

"You can never go wrong doing what God leads you to do."

"I hired a private investigator to look for Janay. It's obvious she doesn't want to be with me, so I want to be released from this marriage so I can move on."

Chapter 16

"Miss Faith, why don't you come to our house anymore?" Nahla inquired as she and her sisters colored at Faith's kitchen table.

"I thought we already talked about that," Faith responded hoping to end the conversation quickly.

"I don't understand why we can't be together anymore."

Faith needed a moment to gather her thoughts and turned to rinse a dish. She had underestimated how difficult it would be to explain so the girls would understand.

"Sometimes adults have to decide what's best. Right now, your dad and I think we need to do things a little differently. No matter what, we're thinking about you, Nia and Naomi."

"But, we don't want what's best. We want things the way they were," Nahla pouted.

"You remember when you went to children's church?"

"Yes."

"Do you remember how they taught you to talk with God?"

"Yes, we can talk to God about anything."

"That's right. We have to remember to ask God to do things the way He wants because God always knows what's best."

"Okay."

"When you pray, I want you to ask God to make things happen the way He wants them to. That way, we'll know it's the right thing."

"But, Miss Faith, I prayed and asked God to send Mommy back and He didn't do that. Does that mean He doesn't want her to come back?

"She didn't come back yet, but she still might."

"I don't want Him to take you away. I'm scared you're going to leave us like Mommy did."

"Don't worry. I won't leave you girls."

Faith continued washing dishes as the girls worked on their pictures. Her mind was spinning from her conversation with Nahla. She hoped she would be able to keep the promise she made to her.

She wanted to see where things went with Evan, but what would happen if Janay returned to reclaim her family? That was a question she didn't want answered.

Chapter 17

"I have to admit I didn't think you would move so fast on this private investigator," Big Momma said.

"I think we all need to know what's going on."

"Are the girls doing better?"

"They miss Janay, but they seem to be getting better. Faith and I try to make sure they have other things to focus on."

"You and Faith, huh?" Evan didn't miss the side-eye Big Momma gave him when he mentioned Faith.

"I hired Jamison Lewis, the guy that has the TV commercials."

"He's supposed to be really good."

"He said he already has some information about Janay. He should be here any minute."

"I hope there's good news about my Janay. I believe she's coming home soon."

Evan didn't respond. If Janay did come home, how would he choose between her and Faith? The doorbell rang causing him to press pause on his thoughts. He opened the door. Jamison Lewis entered wearing a crisp print button down shirt with a leather blazer and denim pants. His polished black leather loafers completed his look.

"This is Jamison Lewis, the private investigator I hired to look for Janay. Jamison, this is my mother-in-law, Leona Miles."

"Wow! You are a lot taller than you look on TV."

Jamison revealed a blinding white smile. "Yes, ma'am. I'm 6-6."

"I'm glad to meet you. My family calls me Big Momma and since you're looking for my Janay that includes you. I hope you have some good news for us. We're all anxious to find my daughter."

"I do have some information about Janay."

"Come on in and have a seat. Can I get you something to drink?" Big Mama inquired.

"No, ma'am. And thank you, but I won't be here that long," he said clasping his hands in front of him.

"Okay, so what have you found?" Evan asked.

"A witness saw your wife with a man about a block away from her workplace the day she disappeared," Jamison reported.

"So what does this mean?" Big Momma questioned no one in particular.

"I think it means my wife lied to me."

"Let's not make any assumptions. Give me some time. I'm certain we will have more information very soon," Jamison spoke confidently. "Mr. Ingram," Jamison shook Evan's hand then turned to Big Momma. "Ma'am," he said with a nod and walked out the door.

Chapter 18

Janay looked around the basement room located in a corner of the house belonging to her coworker and now captor, Frank. The light from two small windows and a light bulb dangling from the ceiling lit the space. The mattress sitting on the floor was her bed. A toilet, sink and shower completed her accommodations.

This had to be a nightmare and she hoped she woke up soon. One moment she was on her way to pick up her daughters from the babysitter's house. The next, she was trapped in Frank's car heading north on Interstate 75 into Oakland County. Frank took good care of her, providing clothing and undergarments. Without her bi-weekly trip to the hair salon, her hair had grown into an afro. Though Frank was a fairly good cook, Janay lost weight worrying about her family and her current living situation.

The sound of Frank's footsteps moving across the floor upstairs alerted her he was heading toward the basement steps. She had been there long enough to discern his footsteps from those of the children that were there from time to time.

"Oh, you're awake," Frank said after he unlocked the door and entered the room. "Would you like to eat? I made some dinner."

"No, but I know what I would like."

"What would that be, darling?"

"I want to go home."

"Won't you miss me if you go home?"

"I'm sorry, Frank, but I really don't know you. So why would I miss you?"

"You do know me. I don't know why you're saying that," he growled as he turned to leave the room, locking the door behind him.

Janay remained quiet after Frank's latest outburst. She didn't know what drove him to do this nor did she know why he was so adamant about their relationship. She didn't want to feed into his belief that she wanted to be there. But, she didn't want to make him angry either since she didn't know if he would become violent. Balancing the two was tricky, particularly considering Frank's apparent mental state.

Not knowing what Frank was capable of doing filled each night away from her family with fear. Evan probably thought she'd left like she told him she wanted to. Janay had wanted space to experience some parts of life she'd missed out on, but not this way.

Chapter 19

Evan and Faith sat across from each other at the smoothie shop trying to decide who would speak first. Since the girls were with their grandmother and aunt, it was the perfect time to discuss their relationship. Evan set his gaze on Faith and quickly removed it once her eyes caught his. This pattern continued until Faith and Evan's eyes locked, refusing to be released.

"What happens next?" Faith broke the silence.

"I don't know. What are your thoughts?"

"We shouldn't be doing this."

"But, it's done. Now the question is where do we go from here?"

"I think it's best if we go back to the way we were. We need to stop spending time together."

"What do you mean?"

"Before Janay left, we engaged in small talk when the girls were dropped off or picked up. Now, we're sitting here talking about a relationship. I think we need to go back to where we made the mistake."

"You want to break up with me?" Evan chuckled.

"I'm saying we need to do the right thing until you and Janay decide what you're going to do with your marriage."

"What marriage?"

"You're married and she could still come back. It would hurt too much if she returned and the two of you just picked up where you left off."

"You should know I've decided to pursue a divorce," Evan said.

"Evan, how are you?" Jamison said as he approached Evan and Faith's table.

"Hey, Jamison," Evan stood to shake the private investigator's hand. "This is the private investigator I hired to find Janay," he said speaking to Faith. "Jamison, this is our babysitter—"

"Faith Richards," Jamison said, completing Evan's introduction.

"Hi, Jamison," Faith whispered, never shifting her gaze from his.

Jamison moved closer to Faith, took her hand and kissed it softly before leaning down to kiss her seductively on her lips.

Shocked, Evan's mouth dropped open as he looked from Jamison to Faith.

"Hey, man. Don't you see me sitting here?"

Jamison studied Evan for a moment. "Excuse me."

"You can't come up in here kissing on my woman like that."

Faith dropped her head in her hands.

"Your woman?" Jamison chuckled. "Faith, what is he talking about?" Faith refused to look up. "Faith and I have been in relationship for a few years," Jamison continued.

"Well, where have you been? She's been spending all of her time with me and my daughters."

"Not that I owe you an explanation, but I've been... I don't know, looking for people like *your wife*. That's where I've been."

Faith sat quietly watching the two men fight over her. In a weird way, it was flattering. She felt eyes on her and noticed the three of them were drawing the attention of several other patrons. She knew she needed to intervene, but she didn't know what to say. Things would get uglier the longer she avoided diffusing the situation. After all, she was at the center of it all. She had to say something before blows were thrown.

"Stop it!" She stood and spoke loudly enough to be heard over their voices.

Both men turned their focus toward her, eyes wide and mouths opened.

"Yes, I'm still here." She waved her hand. "I owe both of you an explanation. Obviously, we can't do it here...together." She waved her hand Vanna White style across the area they were seated in.

She turned to Jamison. "Can you excuse Evan and me?"

"I'm not going anywhere," Jamison said, reaching for a nearby chair.

"I believe you were asked to leave," Evan said. Jamison scowled.

Faith took Jamison's hand, drawing his attention. "We'll have a separate private conversation later. We're probably past due anyway. Please."

"Actually, I'd prefer that." Jamison nodded his head in Evan's direction. "It's none of his business."

"Thank you. I appreciate your understanding."

"You're welcome. I'll call you later, baby." He leaned in and pecked her on the cheek.

Faith nodded her head in agreement. "Okay."

"Evan," Jamison said as he walked away without looking in his direction.

***

After Jamison left, Evan and Faith quietly sipped their beverages. Neither looked at the other.

"What in the world is going on with you and Jamison?"

"What do you want to know?" Faith softly asked.

"From the moment he walked up to the table, you two couldn't tear your eyes away from each other. He kissed you on the lips, then he referred to you as baby, said he's calling you later and you ask me what I want to know?" Evan aggressively questioned.

"Hold on a minute. You really want to question me about my relationship with Jamison?"

"You don't think I have a right to ask considering where our relationship is going?"

Faith's voice rose. "I don't know where it's going. I know what you say now but who's to say what will happen." Faith emphasized her point with an outstretched finger.

Evan sat back in the chair. "Is there something romantic going on between you two?"

"In a way."

"What do you mean...in a way," Evan asked, making quotation marks in the air with his fingers. "Either there is or there isn't." It was Evan's turn to raise his voice.

"Well, I guess the answer is yes."

Evan leaned forward over the table. "Jamison is your boyfriend?"

"Jamison and I were engaged. We didn't get married because I got scared and put things on hold."

"Engaged! You can't still be thinking about marrying him, are you?"

Faith's eyes bucked. "Why not? You're married."

Evan lowered his voice after noticing several patrons staring at them.

"You mean I'm getting ready to divorce my wife for you and you might be marrying Jamison? This is crazy!"

Faith shook her head. "Un, unh. You are not laying this divorce thing on me. That was your idea. I never once asked you to end your marriage. I'm the one saying we need to back this relationship train up. Remember?"

"I can't believe this is happening." Evan rubbed his face with his hands.

Faith stood and moved to Evan's side of the table. "Believe it, Evan Ingram," she spat in response.

Evan stood, matching Faith's level of anger. "What are we doing then?"

Faith shoved her fists into her hips. "I don't know what I'm doing with either of you. But one thing I do know. You will not question me about who I'm seeing or what I'm doing as long as you're married. Have a good day." Faith stormed out of the coffee shop but not before shooting Evan a look over her shoulder.

Chapter 20

Faith looked out of the window once again looking for her visitor to arrive. She was nervous and unsure why. She'd known this man for years and had planned to marry him. She reasoned her trepidation must be because of the uniqueness of the situation and the event at the smoothie shop the previous day. She never stopped loving Jamison and now she had feelings for Evan. Most women would say that was a blessing. For her, it wasn't. She was a one-man woman. She didn't relish the idea of juggling two men at the same time. Her desire was to be fully focused, engaged, and immersed in a relationship with one person at a time.

Finally, she heard what sounded like a car pulling into her driveway. She peeked out, trying not to cause the curtains to move. It was indeed Jamison. She watched as he checked his appearance in the sunshade mirror. He was probably as nervous as she was. He got out of the car wearing dark denim jeans, tan moccasin-style shoes, a tan print shirt and that gleaming smile. She watched him stroll toward her. Watching the way his whole entire body moved was a spiritual experience in itself. It seemed to happen in slow motion so one wouldn't miss a single movement. He was one sexy force of nature.

Gazing at herself in the mirror situated by the front door, she insured her own appearance was as it should be. Faith opened the door and allowed him into her home. He stood in front of her and wrapped her in his arms, without words. There was no place in the world she would rather be in that moment.

"How is my love today?" He asked as her head rose and fell with his chest.

"I am sooo good," she responded, enjoying the physical contact.

They stood for several more moments enjoying each other's presence. Faith didn't realize how much she had missed him.

"Can we sit?" He asked her.

His presence was so overwhelming all she could do was squeak out, "Yes."

The two moved to the couch. He took her hands in his, commanding the attention of her entire being.

"I've missed you, baby," he said.

"I've missed you, too."

"Well, why don't we stop missing each other and just become husband and wife like we planned?"

Faith and Jamison chuckled at the simplicity of his request.

"If only it was that simple."

"It is simple. All you have to do is tell me when and where and we'll make it happen."

"But what about..." Faith started.

Jamison placed a finger over her lips. "This is about us," he said pointing to the two of them.

"You're right." She felt ashamed that she was about to bring up Evan in a discussion with her almost-husband.

"I've been trying to give you some space, Faith, so you could work through this in your own time," Jamison said stroking the back of her hand. "I know you got scared when your parents filed for divorce after we got engaged. But, what I don't understand is how you needing time to think opened the door for you to get involved with somebody else. Can you explain that to me?"

Faith looked away. "Like you said, my parent's situation caused me to take a step back. I mean, if a twenty-plus year marriage like theirs could fail, anybody's could. Then, right after we postponed the wedding, your business took off and you weren't around as much."

Jamison clasped his hands in front of him. "But, we talked about that, love. You told me you understood. I called, sent gifts and we spent time together when I had time. Not once did you tell me this was a major concern for you."

She jutted her chin out. "Well, it was. You didn't spend enough time with me."

Jamison playfully touched her chin and smiled. "I love it when you do that."

"I'm serious, Jamison," she said barely containing a smile.

"But, you never told me that."

"I guess I didn't," she admitted as tears pooled in her eyes.

"How did you get so close to Evan, anyway?"

Faith ran the back of her hand over her eyes. "The girls really missed their mother and I wanted to be there for them. It just seemed like the right thing to do. Spending more time with the girls meant spending more time with Evan, too. That's how this whole thing came about."

Jamison stared out of the adjacent window for a few moments. A look of recognition washed over his face before turning his attention to Faith. "I see now. This is my fault. I should've been more available, even if it meant turning down some business. Because I was missing in action, you filled the void with Evan and his daughters."

Faith thought for a few moments. "Even if that's true, and I'm not sure it is, I've developed a major attachment to Evan."

"Don't you see? You aren't in love with him." Jamison grasped Faith's hands. "Every night I pray God shows you the vision He's shown me for our lives together. I know any minute God is going to do it and I don't want to waste time tying up loose ends with someone else when that happens. I want to be free to be with you."

Faith thought about Jamison's sentiments, carefully rolling them around in her head. This man was working some kind of black man magic on her because she somehow forgot the truth of her feelings for Evan. She knew Jamison was sincere. She knew he was committed to her. But, for some reason she couldn't just forget the Ingrams.

"Where do you stand, Faith? Are you ready to get married now?" Jamison asked looking so intently into her eyes it felt like he was able to view her very soul.

"I don't want to hurt you," she said.

"And I don't want you to hurt me."

"Jamison…"

"Please don't make me beg."

"I love you, Jamison, but I'm involved with someone else."

"Don't throw this relationship away because of infatuation." Jamison stood from his seat, pulling her along with him. He wrapped her in his arms once again and gently planted a kiss on her lips. "Give me a little time to clear up some of my cases. I promise you, there won't be room for Evan Ingram."

Faith savored the sensations this action sent coursing through her body.

"I'm not giving up on us." He exited the house, softly closing the door behind him. Faith couldn't believe she was gambling her future with Jamison for a possibility with Evan. She could only hope she wouldn't regret that decision in the end.

Chapter 21

Janay heard Frank walking toward the stairs. As he descended the stairs, there was something different in the way he moved. She felt a sense of purpose as his feet slammed into the steps. She had heard the children leave the house, presumably for school. Frank entered her line of sight. Janay knew something was different and she braced herself for what she feared was to come.

"Janay, I've been thinking about us."

"I'm a married woman, Frank. There is no us," Janay said pointing between the two of them.

"He doesn't love you like I do."

"Look, I know we went to lunch a few times, but we're just coworkers."

"We are not just coworkers," Frank spoke through gritted teeth. He slammed his clinched fists into the cement wall. The veins in his head and neck jumped to attention with his mounting rage.

Janay tried to figure out whether she should continue trying to convince Frank this love relationship he thought they had didn't exist. It was obvious he was mentally unstable, but she didn't see a reason to pretend their relationship was something it wasn't. He needed to know she didn't feel the same way about him. She had tried to tell him so in many different ways, but he still didn't get it. She decided to try logic this time, hoping he would finally understand.

"If I wanted to be here, you wouldn't have to lock me in the basement to make me stay."

Janay saw the wheels turning as his facial expression changed. It was clear realization had set in. She hoped it wouldn't make him any angrier.

"You're just trying to hurt me. I know you love me and I love you. We'll never be apart again."

"You can't possibly love me and I'm not in love with you."

"I do love you and I'm going to show you how much," Frank said as he moved swiftly toward her. He kissed her hard in the mouth, attempting to pry her lips open to insert his tongue. Refusing to allow his tongue to enter her mouth, Janay pressed her lips together tightly. He moaned and backed away with a lustful look in his eyes.

Frank chuckled. "I can do rough."

With both hands, Frank grabbed her t-shirt and tore it away from her body. Next, his hand gripped the center of her bra and snatched it off. Janay gasped, realizing Frank's intent.

Janay attempted to cover her bare breasts, moving deeper into the room. "Please don't do this to me. If you love me like you say you do, you wouldn't do this,"

Frank approached her, hungrily eyeing her body. "This is going to be great."

He grabbed her shoulders and grunted as he tossed her on to the makeshift bed. Her knees and fists flailed as he moved toward her. Her knee connected with his middle. He moaned briefly but kept moving.

She continued throwing her fists and legs. He gained control of her arms, pinned them over her head and suckled her breasts.

Janay struggled under his weight as he laid on top of her. "No, stop. I don't want this."

"Oh, you don't like that?" Frank surmised. "Let me try something else, baby. I want to make you feel good. Don't move."

Frank released Janay's hands. He straddled her ankles. Then, began pulling her pants down. Janay screamed. She swung at Frank and stung the side of his head as she sat up, attempting to keep him from reaching his goal.

Frank smacked the side of Janay's face. "Didn't I tell you not to move?"

Startled, Janay's hand flew to her face. She laid back on the bed.

Frank pulled her pants the rest of the way off along with her underwear, leaving Janay completely naked. He then stood to undress himself. He removed his shirt in a strip-tease fashion while maintaining eye contact with the teary-eyed Janay.

"Don't cry, honey. I wanted to wait until we got married, but I don't think God will mind if we do this now."

"You're right, honey." Janay got up from the bed and stood in front of Frank. "I guess I should stop fighting our love. It's so strong I can't even stand it."

"Yeah, that's what I'm talking about." He undid the waist of his pants and began to lower them down his legs.

Janay took hold of Frank's hands before he completed the task. She looked into his eyes. She lightly bit his bottom lip, backing away a little as a smile spread across her face. She slowly leaned forward, her lips almost touching his. Then, she pushed him with every bit of strength she had causing him to lose his balance. She took off out of the room. Janay was within reach of the door at the top of the stairs when Frank grabbed her and carried her back into the room.

"No! Please don't do this!" She pleaded with her captor. Though she continued pleading, kicking and punching, it seemed to have no effect.

"Oh, you want me to chase you? That's a fun idea, but not for our first time. I'm going to make love to you like you've never been loved before." Frank laid a resigned Janay on the comforter he'd provided for her. He positioned himself over her and roughly joined himself with her. She squirmed from the pain and Frank mistook it for enjoyment.

"Ah, this is wonderful. I love the way you move. I knew when we finally came together it was going to be amazing. This is beyond what I thought it would be."

Janay allowed Frank to continue as she lay underneath him and sobbed. How could he be so oblivious to her deep sadness?

Would she ever get out of here or would she spend the rest of her life being Frank's make-believe wife?

Chapter 22

"I have some more information about Janay's disappearance," Jamison announced as he entered Big Momma's house.

"Come on in and have a seat. You want something to eat? I made some lasagna," Big Momma offered.

"It smells wonderful, but I don't think I should. Don't let me stop you two, though."

"You're family now, so it's required. Do you want salad and garlic bread, too? Never mind. I'll just get you some."

"I don't think he has time for dinner, Big Momma. Right Jamison?" Evan glared at Jamison.

"He's got time. Can I get you some sweet tea?" Big Momma went toward the kitchen.

"Yes, please," Jamison responded.

The three sat down and Big Momma blessed the meal. After a few moments, Evan asked for the update.

"I have some pictures of your wife and the man people saw her with. I want you to take a look and see if you know him." He opened the case containing his tablet so he could play the video. The two watched as Janay and the man walked past a camera located a few doors down from where Janay worked. She seemed to be enjoying the conversation immensely.

"Do either of you recognize this man?" Jamison asked.

Big Momma and Evan shook their heads.

"I think this may be our guy. This guy and Janay were seen together quite often. He's a contractor where your wife works. Apparently, his last day of work there was the day Janay disappeared."

"Well, why aren't we out there arresting him?"

"Arrest him for what? We don't know if he committed a crime. It's possible Janay left willingly."

"I guess you're right. She sure doesn't appear to be in trouble."

After their meal, Big Momma stood, gathering dishes from the table.

Jamison stood and took the plates from her hands. "Let me help you with these."

"I appreciate your offer, but I can take care of these few dishes."

"In that case, I'll be leaving now. The lasagna was outstanding. I really enjoyed it. I'll be in touch with you two soon." Jamison rose and exited the house.

Evan rose and followed Jamison outside. As the two approached Jamison's car, he asked, "Hey, uh, Jamison. You got a minute?"

"Sure," Jamison responded.

Evan focused his attention downward as he spoke. "I don't think you're the right private investigator for this case anymore." He looked up at Jamison.

"Why not? I'm one of the best private investigators out there. That's why you called me."

"Let's just say I changed my mind."

"Is this because of Faith?"

"Yes. I think it would be best if I found someone else."

Jamison nodded then rubbed his chin for a moment. "If you want to hire someone else, that's your prerogative. I'll invoice you for the outstanding balance and we can conclude our business. I feel the need to remind you I'm a professional. This personal stuff won't change how I approach this case at all if you decide to continue working with me. Regardless of your decision, it won't affect Faith and I. I'll wait to hear from you regarding your decision," Jamison declared as he got in his car to leave the property.

***

Big Momma watched as Evan and Jamison ended their conversation. Both men's facial expression said they were angry. Evan walked toward the house as Jamison entered his car and backed out of the driveway.

"That was a pretty intense conversation you had with Jamison," Big Momma spoke as Evan re-entered her home.

"Yes, it was. I think I'm going to fire him."

"We were just sitting here eating lasagna and talking. What happened that quickly?"

"Don't worry, Big Momma. We're still going to keep looking for Janay."

"Is it because of the money? You know I can help pay for the investigation."

"No, it's not money."

"Well, what is it? It doesn't make sense to start all over again with somebody new."

"I don't want to discuss it."

"No, you're going to have to tell me why you're firing him."

Evan exhaled and stated, "He was engaged to Faith."

"So..." Big Momma moved her hands in a circular motion, urging Evan to continue.

"I think it's a conflict of interest."

"Whose interest?"

"I knew you wouldn't understand. That's why I didn't want to discuss it with you."

"You didn't want to discuss this with me because you know you're wrong."

"Wrong?"

"Yes, wrong. Jamison and Faith are well within their rights to do whatever they please and you have no right to interfere."

"I'm pursuing a relationship with Faith so I have every right to get involved."

"You are still married to my daughter so you shouldn't be pursuing a relationship with anybody."

"I respect your opinion, but I still think it's best for me to hire someone else."

"So you're willing to jeopardize the search for my daughter because Faith is involved with Jamison. I'm starting to wonder if you really want to find Janay."

Evan dropped his head and stuffed his hands in his pockets. "That hurts. I do want to find her."

"It hurts me to say it, but your focus is off and we don't have time for this drama. This is why you had no business getting involved with Faith in the first place. Now, you can fire Jamison if you want to, but I'll just rehire him. I like him and I think he's doing a good job."

Chapter 23

Janay paced the floor, thinking about the predicament she was in. She regretted trusting Frank even after she knew he was acting strangely. If she hadn't gotten into his car, she wouldn't be sitting in this cold basement unsure of her future.

She no longer knew how long she'd been held in the basement. Once the count reached a hundred days, she stopped counting the sunrises and sunsets she witnessed through the small window. Too much time had passed since she'd seen her Ns. It had been too long since she'd been in Evan's arms and felt the love no one else could give her except him.

She prayed Evan wouldn't give up hope on her and their marriage. She asked God to watch over each of her loved ones and to somehow let them know she loved them and hadn't abandoned them.

Janay heard the door leading to the basement open. The footsteps of the smaller child descended the stairs. Though she'd never seen either of the children, she knew their footsteps intimately. She heard the soft thud of small feet approaching the room she was being kept in. The door slowly creaked open. Janay braced herself for another encounter with Frank. Instead, the sweetest face Janay ever saw, aside from her Ns, peered around the door. He wore a striped t-shirt, blue jeans and nothing on his feet. Janay decided to engage her unexpected visitor since the only person she ever saw was Frank.

She stood and approached the child. "Hi. What's your name?"

The child responded with a huge smile. "Trey."

"That's a nice name. Come talk to me," Janay took the child's hand and slowly led him into the room.

Trey hesitated as he sat on the mattress. He looked around as if he'd never been in this part of the house.

"Do you go to school?"

"Nope."

"Where's your mommy?"

Trey shrugged his shoulders.

"Is your daddy here?" Janay figured she might as well get some information about her captor's whereabouts.

"I don't have no daddy."

If he wasn't their father, then who was Frank to them?

"Trey!" A voice called out for her visitor.

"Is that your sister?" Janay asked.

"Bye," Trey said as he disappeared up the stairs.

"It was nice of you to visit me," Janay said as she waved at the youngster. "I can't wait until you come back again."

Janay wondered how the child got into the normally locked room. She hoped he would return. He just might be her way out of this place.

Chapter 24

Evan walked up the stairs to Faith's front door. He reached the top and overheard her speaking with his daughters. He smiled as he heard her getting them ready to leave.

"Miss Faith, I talked to God just like you told me to," Nahla reported.

"You did?"

"Uh huh. I think you can come back now," the little girl stated.

"Really? What makes you think that?"

"God said so."

Evan decided to rescue Faith from this conversation. He rang the doorbell and waited for the door to open.

"Hi. They're all ready to go," Faith said as she let out a huge breath and began pushing the girls out the front door.

"What about movie night tonight? You can pick the movie." Nahla was persistent in her desire for more of Faith's presence.

"I don't think so, Nahla."

Evan laughed and nudged the girls back inside. "Girls, can you go play for a couple of minutes so Miss Faith and I can talk?"

"Okay, Daddy," Nia said as the three girls left the room.

"So, how have you been?" Evan asked Faith who seemed out of sorts.

"I'm fine."

"It's been a while."

"I know. It's what we agreed to though."

"That doesn't mean we can't change the agreement."

"I know."

"I've missed you and I know the girls do, too. Why don't you come over tonight? We'll have a taco bar and we'll watch whatever movie you like just like Nahla said."

"I've missed being with you all too. I'm just trying to protect my heart, you know. I'm scared of my feelings." Faith fell into Evan's arms. Soon, Evan felt wetness on his chest and realized she was crying. "I don't know what to do," Faith whispered into his chest.

"Please come. We'll talk after the girls go to bed. Since it'll be late, you can just stay over in the guest room if you like."

Faith pulled herself from Evan's arms and wiped her face. "I don't think so, Evan. I think it's best if I don't."

"I promise it'll be okay."

"Okay, I'll come. Just know this is against my better judgment though."

***

"Mommy," a young voice screamed in the middle of the night.

Faith rose from the bed in the Ingram's guest room, grabbed her robe and ran into the hall.

"Come back!" The voice continued to yell.

Faith ran trying to get to the distressed child. When she got to the end of the hallway, Evan appeared from the master bedroom. Faith stopped as Evan's eyes roamed over her body. Faith looked down and realized she had neglected to adequately cover herself in her haste to see which one of the girls needed attention. She slowly grabbed the collar of her robe and attempted to pull it up around her neck to cover herself from Evan's gaze. He gently pulled the fabric from her hand exposing her cleavage once again. Evan and Faith stood face-to-face waiting to see what the other would do. Evan leaned into Faith who responded in kind. But, Nahla came running out of the bedroom into her father's arms before their lips could touch. Faith took a step back, pulled her robe closed and tightened the sash around her waist.

"What's wrong, baby? You were screaming," Evan asked his daughter while keeping his eyes on Faith.

"I had a nightmare about Mommy," she said looking between Evan and Faith as if sensing their connection. "Can I sleep with you, Daddy?"

"Yes, but only for tonight. Tell Miss Faith good night."

"Good night, honey. I'll see you in the morning." Faith hugged Nahla and shot Evan a look.

"I knew this was a bad idea," she whispered. Evan smirked and led Nahla into the master bedroom.

***

Evan sat on the side of the bed. He couldn't sleep thinking about what almost happened between him and Faith. The attraction was palpable. He looked over at a snoring Nahla and smiled. If it hadn't been for her running into the hall, he wasn't sure what would have transpired. Perhaps, Faith was right. It wasn't such a good idea for her to be down the hall wearing that gown with the neckline showing off just a peek of her cleavage. He fought to stay in his room instead of heading down the hall to the guest room. He wanted her. Badly. He laid down and covered himself with the quilt. If he could get his mind off the woman in the guest room, perhaps he could fall asleep. Meanwhile, he would have to remind himself a sexual relationship with Faith was something that would have to wait. If he pressed the issue, she might never return and he didn't want to scare her off. He wanted to keep her around as much as possible.

***

Faith leaned against the closed bedroom door. Still clutching the gown around her neck, she struggled to calm her breathing. After a few moments, she removed the robe and sat on the bed.

Her cell phone notified her of a text message. She viewed the screen. Jamison. Without opening the text, she read the message.

I'm thinking about you, baby.

Faith read the message a few times before placing the phone back on the nightstand and settled in the bed. Ironically, Faith had been dreaming about Jamison before being awakened. Now, her mind was on the man down the hall.

Chapter 25

Janay sat on the mattress with her knees under her chin and tried to stay focused. Each day she spent locked in the basement made it more difficult to remain positive, but she knew falling apart would not solve the problem. Frank's resolve didn't seem to be weakening. He believed she was his wife and his intention was to keep her there forever.

The sound of someone handling the locks that secured the door to the room she was in interrupted her thoughts. She braced herself in preparation for Frank's entrance. She never knew what kind of mood he might be in so she had to prepare for anything.

The door opened, and Trey and his sister, ten year-old Deasia, entered the room.

"Hurry. Close the door," Janay said. She didn't want anyone to know the kids were in her room. She relaxed a little. They had been visiting for a few weeks and Janay enjoyed the interaction. "Are you here alone?"

"Yes," Trey responded.

"I'm glad you two came to see me. It gets lonely down here."
She embraced her visitors.

Frank's footsteps startled the trio. "Oh, no! Frank can't find
you here." Janay pointed the children toward the foot of the
mattresses. Though the children quickly followed her direction, it
was too late.

"What are you kids doing down here?" Frank's voice bounced
off the concrete walls in the small room.

"We just came to visit. That's all," Deasia whined.

"Didn't I tell you not to come down here?"

"Yes," both children replied.

"You know what to do. Bend over and grab your ankles,"
Frank demanded.

"Leave them alone. They didn't do anything wrong," Janay
cried.

"You better do what I said. Now," Frank yelled, wagging a
pointed finger at the children.

Both children slowly bent over waiting for their punishment.
Janay moved between Frank and the children, protecting them
from the pain Frank hoped to inflict.

"You'd better move or you'll be next," Frank said as he
pushed her out of the way. Janay pushed him back, intent on
keeping him from hitting Trey and Deasia.

"What does it hurt for them to talk to me, anyway?" She
questioned, continuing to wrestle with Frank.

"Because you're mine and I'm not going to share you." Frank
seethed. Janay wasn't sure if he was more upset because the
children disobeyed him or because she was interfering.

"I'm not yours. You only think I am," she shot back.

Frank pulled his fist back and punched Janay square in the jaw, throwing her against the concrete wall. She attempted to regain her balance. He followed with a blow to her other jaw causing her to lose her balance and hit her head on the sink. Everything went black.

***

Janay turned over in her bed and moaned from the pain the small movement inflicted upon her. The left side of her face felt numb. The right side of her head hurt so badly she was sure her skull was cracked. Every inch of her torso was sore. She lifted her top and noted the bruising. That explained the pain but not what caused it.

She sat on the side of the bed and allowed the dam of emotions to break. Janay had expended so much energy trying to stay strong and not lose her mind. But this beating was challenging her resolve. She was about to surrender when a vision of her Ns floated through her mind. She wished she could be home sitting on the couch watching silly movies and eating popcorn with her family. She would give anything to be cuddled up with Evan, telling him how much she loved him and how sorry she was for even suggesting a separation. What had she been thinking?

Her desire for an adult timeout had dissipated. At the time, all she wanted was some space to regroup. She was burned out from working full-time along with being a wife and mother. She'd had enough of picking up toys and shoes and cleaning up after every one. She longed to have some fun, to rediscover the Janay she lost in the mound of laundry and meal preparation. None of those things mattered now. She never should've even entertained the thought of leaving her family. This was her punishment for doing so and she deserved it.

She gave herself a few more moments to experience these sad emotions. She felt she was entitled to them. Then, she wiped her eyes and cancelled the pity party. She had a decision to make. She had to either figure out how to get out of this predicament or prepare to die. Those were her only options. If she gave up now, she might as well expect the latter.

Janay felt a strong urge to do something she hadn't done in a while and decided to follow it. She got on her knees and prayed. In that moment, she released everything that was on her heart. It seemed like hours passed before she said amen, but she felt refreshed. Refilled. The cloud of depression began to dissipate. For the first time since she'd been locked in the basement and held by a crazy man, she felt hopeful.

Chapter 26

Janay heard the children descending the stairs. She hadn't seen them since the day Frank attacked her, breaking her jaw and giving her a black eye. She heard a woman's voice also.

"I'm going to have to talk to Uncle Frank about what he's letting you guys watch on TV. There is no woman in this house."

"There is a lady here. I'm not lying," Trey said.

"Okay, where is she then?" The woman asked.

"She's over here in this room, Mommy." This time it was Deasia who spoke.

Janay was concerned about this woman who apparently was the children's mother, at least that's what they called her.

"Right here," Trey said.

"What's in here that requires all these locks? How am I supposed to get in here?" She asked as she fumbled with the chains and locks.

"There's some keys over there by the heater. Uncle Frank told us to never bother those."

"You didn't follow directions did you?" Deasia asked.

"You didn't either!" Trey responded.

"He didn't tell me not to bother them. He told you," Deasia claimed.

"Yes, he did!" Trey yelled.

"Kids! Stop all that fussing."

The woman found the keys and unlocked the locks. She opened the door slowly. Janay stood ready to defend herself. The lady was tall and thin with a short afro, cocoa brown skin, and a strong angular jawline. She had bright eyes like Frank.

"Oh, my goodness. Who are you?"

Janay moved deeper into the room unsure of the woman.

"Don't be afraid. I'm Vonne. Frank's sister."

Janay remained silent, plotting her next move.

"'Are you okay? Did Frank do this to you?" The woman asked looking closely at Janay's face. "My kids have been telling me there was a woman down here for a few weeks, but I didn't believe them. Trey, go get my phone."

Still unsure about where the woman stood and who she was going to call, Janay ran from the room. The woman and children followed behind her trying to catch her. Janay kept running until she found a door.

"It's okay. I'm trying to get some help," Vonne yelled.

Janay kept running, choosing to take a chance on finding a stranger to help her rather than this woman. For all she knew, Vonne may have known Frank had her down there the whole time.

Janay ran, ducking between houses, until she spotted a small strip mall about three blocks away. She ran into the dry cleaners and asked them to call the police.

***

Frank spotted Janay running down Franklin Road on his way home and knew he was in trouble. He immediately did a U-turn to catch up with her. He lost track of her but knew she ran into the small shopping plaza on the corner. There were five different businesses located in the plaza so it would only take a few minutes to figure out where she was. Determined to find her and return her to their home, Frank drove slowly by each shop looking for her. He spotted her in the dry cleaners, parked his car and ran inside.

"Baby, what are you doing here?" He asked.

"This is the man that kidnapped me!" Janay spoke, moving away from her captor.

"Sir, we called the police."

"My wife is mentally ill and apparently she didn't take her medication today. I'm very sorry for this. I'll just take her home."

Janay frantically shook her head and backed away from Frank who was moving toward her.

"Come on, honey. It's going to be okay," Frank said reaching for her.

Janay escaped his reach, ran behind the counter and hid behind a female employee. She caught sight of herself in a mirror and realized she did look like someone who was not in their right mind. Her face was badly bruised. Her hair was flying all over her head and the parts of her eyes that were visible beyond the swelling were red. She feared people would believe Frank.

Frank ran behind the counter, knocked the female employee down and grabbed Janay around her middle, lifting her from the floor.

"What are you doing?" Frank whispered to Janay as he carried her toward the door. "You can't leave me. We're going to be together forever. Remember?"

"No! Don't let him take me!" Janay kicked and screamed as he carried her toward the door. Her sobs were interrupted by the arrival of a police officer.

"Did someone here call the police?"

"Oh, thank God you're here," Janay said, stopping her assault on Frank.

"Yes, we called you because this woman said she was in trouble and needed help," another employee offered.

"Officer, my wife is a mental patient and I don't think she took her medication today. Everything will be fine once I get her home," Frank said to the cop.

"Sir, I need you to let this woman go and stand over there while I get some information," the officer said pointing to the counter. The officer turned her attention to Janay. "I'm Officer Johnson, ma'am. How can I assist you?"

Janay ran toward the officer once Frank released her. "I'm Janay Ingram and this man kidnapped me."

Officer Johnson gazed at Frank who responded by shaking his head and circling his index finger around his temple.

"What is your date of birth, Miss Ingram?"

"November 29, 1990."

"Officer Johnson to dispatch. I'm here on a call. I'm secure but I need another unit. I'm dealing with a possible 027 and 207." She glanced at Janay. "But I'm still gaining more information."

"I don't know what you told them but I'm not mentally ill like he said," Janay explained.

"Ma'am, let's go out to my vehicle so I can find out what's going on here."

"I'm being arrested? Why aren't you taking *him* to your car? He's the one who should be arrested." Janay began crying hysterically.

Frank folded his arms as he leaned back against the counter, shaking his head. "She gets bad when she doesn't take those pills, but I've never seen her this bad. Her doctor might need to adjust the dosage," Frank mentioned to no one in particular. "It's okay, baby," He said turning back to Janay. "We'll get you all taken care of when we get home."

The officer addressed Janay, "Ma'am, I just need you to calm down. You are not under arrest. I have to verify your identity and then you can tell me what's going on."

"I'm the victim!" Janay shrieked. "I'm not going to your car, Officer Johnson or whatever your name is."

"I certainly can't force you, Ma'am. But, I do need you to come with me so I can help you. Don't you want to call your family and let them know you're okay? We can sort this out quickly if you cooperate."

Janay thought about the officer's proposition. She did want to be reunited with her family.

"I'll come with you, but what about him?"

"My partner should be here shortly to speak with him."

Frank began to pace the floor.

Janay moved toward the exit and stopped at the door to the police vehicle.

"Ma'am, I'm going to have to pat you down first. Do you have any weapons, needles or anything I need to be aware of?"

"I can't handle being touched. He's been molesting me for months!"

"It's for your safety and mine. Don't worry. I'll be respectful but I need you to put your hands on the hood of the car and spread your legs a little."

"You don't understand what I've been through. There must be another way. Why can't I stand in the drycleaners and you put him in the car?"

"If you want me to help you, this is how we have to do it. Remember, I'm trying to get this resolved and get you back to your family as quickly as possible."

Janay yielded, placing her hands on the vehicle. Her breath quickened as she anticipated the officer's hands roaming her body. Her body stiffened and she couldn't seem to catch her breath.

"I can't breathe!" She cried as the officer touched her breasts and grazed other areas of her body. Once the search was over, Janay worked to calm herself and slow her breathing.

"Are you okay?" Officer Johnson asked.

"No, but I'll be better once I get home to my family," Janay said wiping her tears away with the back of her hand.

Janay looked up and noticed Frank getting into his car. Through her tears, she yelled, "He's getting away while you're arresting me! Don't let him get away!"

"Sir, I need you to stay."

Frank turned toward Officer Johnson. "Am I under arrest?"

"No, sir. But, we need to get this cleared up."

"If I'm not under arrest, then I'm leaving."

"Ma'am, I'm going to place you in the car now."

After assisting Janay so she wouldn't bump her head getting into the car, the officer reached for her two-way radio. "Officer Johnson to dispatch, male subject driving a blue SUV traveling north on Telegraph Road from westbound Square Lake Road."

A look of recognition washed over Janay's face. "Oh my God, you believe him don't you? You think I'm crazy because what he said makes sense when you look at my appearance. I have been locked in his basement for I don't know how many months. This is my first breath of fresh air in all of that time. He raped me and beat me. I didn't know if I would ever get out of there. Does anyone escape a situation like that looking…normal? I assure you, Officer, I am not insane and he certainly isn't my husband. In his mind, he thinks he is. Now, I want to call my real husband like you promised."

"I'm going to check your identity and see if you've been reported missing."

"Okay." Janay's mind raced as she realized this would all soon be over and she would be back home with Evan and her Ns. Surely her family reported her missing or maybe they hadn't because she'd wanted to walk away for a time.

Her mind refocused on Trey and Deasia. She was thankful they indirectly helped her escape. At the same time, she'd seen how angry Frank could become when things didn't go his way. She knew he was capable of physical retaliation and was worried about the price they might have to pay because they unwittingly helped her get away.

"The system is down so I can't verify your information at this time. We're going to have to go to the station to figure everything out."

"Meanwhile, Frank is probably halfway to Timbuktu by now. This is ridiculous."

Chapter 27

Faith walked around Evan's kitchen preparing sandwiches for the Ns. Evan ran out, after receiving a phone call, but would be returning soon. She cut each sandwich in quarters for the girls, added a few baby carrots and set the plates on the table.

"Lunch is ready. Wash your hands and come on down," she yelled at the girls, while pouring juice in small cups for them. She decided to wait for Evan so they could have lunch together.

She and Evan had fallen into a comfortable rhythm as a family unit. She came in the morning to get Nahla and Nia ready for school, cared for Naomi during the day, picked the girls up from school and prepared dinner. Once dinner was done and the children settled in for the night, Faith went home. Some nights she stayed overnight in the Ingram's guest room. She usually spent the weekends doing fun things with Evan and the girls. In her rare free time, she spent most of it catching up with her life. Faith felt this was where she belonged, though she was still insecure. Evan said he wanted to find Janay and end their marriage. However, she was a little unsure whether Evan would follow through with it if he actually located her.

"You're not eating, Miss Faith?" Nahla asked.

"I'm going to eat with your dad. I don't know where he went, but I thought he'd be back by now."

"It's a secret, but I know where he went," Nahla sang.

"How do you know where he went?" Faith playfully asked, not taking Nahla seriously.

"I was listening when he was talking to Big Momma," Nahla reported.

"Okay, so where did he go?"

"He said he didn't want you to know because you might get upset," Nahla said as she adjusted the bread on a quarter of her sandwich.

Faith leaned over the counter overlooking the kitchen nook. "What did he think I would be upset about?"

"Somebody called about Mommy and Daddy's going to get her."

"Really?" Faith straightened her body and looked at the ceiling.

"Yes, and that means we can all be together again just like before. Aren't you excited, Miss Faith?"

Faith's heart hit her feet with a thump. Maybe Nahla didn't hear correctly. No, it couldn't be true. Surely, Evan would have told her. But, what if it was true? What then? She decided she wouldn't allow her mind to go there unless it was necessary. "Yes, I'm really excited."

Chapter 28

"You'll notice her external wounds right away. Her physical recovery is overshadowed by her mental and emotional recovery. We know she has been physically and sexually assaulted. I want you to be aware of what your wife has been through so you won't be shocked by how she might react," the doctor stated as he walked beside Evan.

Evan listened intently to the doctor, trying to grasp every detail of what he said. He didn't want to think about the treatment Janay endured.

The doctor stopped in front of the room Janay was in. "Are you ready?" He asked with a sympathetic smile.

"Yes, I need to see her."

The door opened and there she was. Janay. Even with all of the bruises and swelling, he recognized her. He moved without realizing he did so and found himself at her side. He carefully sat on the side of the bed, trying not to cause her more pain.

"Janay. Baby. I'm here," Evan said as he inspected her injuries.

"I'll come back in a little while," the doctor stated as he exited. "By the way, who are the Ns? That's all she's been talking about. Her Ns."

Evan chuckled as he realized Janay had them on her mind the entire time. Of course, the Ns would be her main concern. "They're our three daughters. Their names begin with N."

"I was just curious. We figured it was important."

As he sat there holding Janay's hand, his cell phone vibrated in his pocket. He pulled it out with his free hand and looked at the caller ID. It was Faith. It occurred to him how much trouble he was in. He had finally found his wife so he could divorce her and now he wasn't sure that's what he wanted to do. After all, she hadn't abandoned them as he thought and she'd endured so much. Knowing this made him love her even more. He wanted to be with her and help her through this.

He was thinking about this dilemma when Janay moved. Her eyes popped open and her breath quickened. She looked around the room like a frightened animal. A layer of sweat formed on her face. Evan didn't quite know what to do, so he decided to wait to see what would happen. Finally, she discovered him sitting there. She reached for him and he surrounded her with his arms. With what seemed to be an endless stream of tears, she sobbed on his shoulder. Evan cried too but for different reasons. He knew something she didn't. Someone was going to get hurt.

Chapter 29

Frank carefully observed his surroundings to insure no one had followed him home. To be certain, he'd driven to Flint and back a couple of times. He pulled into the attached garage and pressed the button to lower the door before exiting his vehicle.

He rushed into the kitchen from the garage and breathed a sigh of relief. He relaxed against the counter, willing his heart rate to return to normal.

"I've been waiting on you." Frank jumped upon hearing the unexpected voice. "You seem a little nervous. What's wrong?"

"Nothing. Everything's good. What are you doing here?"

"I needed to check on you and see what's going on," Vonne stated.

"Everything is good."

"Hmm, I see. So, who was the woman in your basement?" Vonne asked entering the kitchen and leaning against the pantry door.

"What woman?"

"Don't play with me, Frank. I found her locked in the room in your basement."

"I don't know what you're talking about."

"I saw her with my own eyes so you can stop denying it."

"How did you find out?"

"Deasia and Trey told me about her. Why was she here?"

"God gave her to me. He said she was my wife."

"Aren't you still married to Tachelle?"

"Who?"

"Your wife, Tachelle Scott."

"Don't ever mention that woman's name to me again," Frank yelled as he pounded his fist into the counter.

"Why? Because she was tired of you flipping out and hitting her or because she left you?"

"No, because she left me for another man."

"You always said that, but she told me there was never anyone else."

"And you believe her, don't you?"

"Yes, I do. But, let's get back to the subject at hand. Why did you have that woman locked in your basement?"

"I finally found someone who really loves me and wants to be with me. That's all I ever wanted."

"I don't think she wanted to be here. She ran out of here so fast, I couldn't catch her."

"What did you do to make her leave?"

"Me?"

"What did you tell her? You had to tell her something to make her leave me."

"I didn't have time to say anything."

"Why did you have to mess things up for us? You're just jealous because Malik left you and the kids. I bet you had something to do with Tachelle leaving, too," Frank accused.

"This has nothing to do with me and you know it. That woman in your basement had bruises all over her face and I know you're responsible for every one of them. You need to accept that she didn't want to be your wife and she is not coming back. In fact, you probably need to pull yourself together so you can deal with the police."

Frank's demeanor changed. "Did you call the police on me? I knew you could be low down and dirty, but I can't believe you would call the police on your own brother."

"I can't believe what you did to that woman and just so you know, I didn't call the police but I'm sure she did by now."

"Get out of my house and don't ever come back."

"That's not going to fix this. You are angry and delusional. I've been begging you for years to see a doctor about what's going on with you. Now, you got yourself in a mess and you want to blame me for it."

"I said get out!" Frank screamed, reaching into his pocket and pulling out a small handgun.

"Really? You going to shoot me because I'm saying what you don't want to hear?"

"Are you walking out or will you be carried out?"

"I'll leave," Vonne said as she pulled her purse up on her shoulder. "Please think about turning yourself in. Otherwise, this could end badly."

Frank aimed his gun directly at Vonne, drawing a gasp. She walked toward her brother and attempted to embrace him. After hearing the bullet load into the chamber, she dropped her hands and with a shake of her head, walked around him to exit the house.

"I never want to see you again," Frank yelled, still waving the gun at her. "I mean it. You've ruined my life for the last time."

Vonne paused at the door. With her back to Frank, she said, "You know in your heart I've never done anything to hurt you. I love you, Frank."

She exited the home, hoping Frank would listen to her and not resist the police. Vonne didn't even want to imagine what might happen if he didn't.

Chapter 30

Faith wiped down the kitchen counters for what seemed like the hundredth time. She couldn't help herself. Though she promised herself she wouldn't worry until she knew there was a reason to, she was breaking that promise. She was scared.

The rumble of footsteps coming from upstairs shook Faith from her thoughts. She heard Evan enter the house. Nahla and Nia must've heard him too because the girls and Evan appeared in the living room at the same time. His facial expression said Janay was found. Hers told him she knew.

"Daddy, where's Mommy?" Nia asked her father, wrapping her arms around him as far as they could reach.

"Who said anything about Mommy?"

"Nahla said she heard you say you were going to get her."

"Well, I did see her," Evan's eyes were glued to Faith's.

"Yay!" Nahla and Nia yelled. Nahla ran to Faith and hugged her stiff body. "Aren't you excited, Miss Faith?

"Um, yes. Yes, of course I'm excited." Faith felt bad for lying to Nahla, but it wouldn't be fair to say, *No, I'm not excited. I was hoping your mommy stayed away because her return complicates things.*

"Mommy asked about you girls."

"Where is she?" Nia asked looking toward the door.

"The doctors have to help her get better before she can come home."

Faith felt like she was suffocating. She needed to get out of this house. If she didn't, she might pass out or throw up or both. Picking up her purse, she headed past Evan toward the front door. She slid her feet into her shoes and turned toward the Ingrams.

"I've got to run. I'll see you guys later," she announced.

"Girls, can you go upstairs for a few minutes? I need to talk to Miss Faith," Evan said.

"No," Faith said putting her palms out. "You all should be celebrating. We'll talk later."

Once outside, Faith took a couple of deep breaths. She got into her car and started the engine. She rounded the corner and put the car in park, releasing the sounds and tears that expressed her pain. She thought she had found her happy place with Evan and the girls. Would she lose the sense of family she had developed with them? It would take time for her to find that out. Until then, she would have to protect herself from further disappointment. As she shifted the car into gear, she realized she should have been doing that all along.

***

Evan finally got the girls settled from the excitement of the day. He sat on the side of the bed and exhaled. Though he'd hoped and prayed for this day, he didn't expect the clash of emotions he experienced.

Seeing Janay in the condition she was in softened his feelings toward her. Another man had brutalized his wife in ways he never imagined. If he could, he would take every bit of pain she experienced onto himself.

Evan picked up the phone to call Faith for the tenth time. Like every attempt before, his call went straight to voicemail. He shouldn't be surprised. He was sure Faith was processing Janay's return just as he was. He wanted to reassure her his feelings for her hadn't changed.

After seeing and finding out what happened to Janay, the future of his relationship with Faith was unclear. The truth was he wanted them both, but he knew that wasn't possible. How would he choose?

***

Faith reviewed her missed calls and noticed the latest call she received was from Evan just like the last several. She wasn't sure whether she was ready to talk to him. Her phone's voicemail tone rang out. Undoubtedly, Evan had left another message for her. Since it was obvious he wasn't giving up, she decided to face him rather than continue delaying the inevitable. She picked up her cell phone and returned Evan's call.

111

"Thank you for returning my phone call," Evan said once he answered.

"You're welcome."

The awkwardness of the moment led to a pause in the conversation.

"Faith, I don't want anything to change between you and me."

"There's no way things won't change."

"We don't have to let that happen."

"What are you going to do when Janay gets out of the hospital? Huh? Tell her she has to find someplace else to live?"

"I haven't thought that far ahead."

"But I have and this probably won't end well for me."

"Please don't shut me out. I don't think I can take it," Evan said as his voice quivered.

Faith sensed the emotion in Evan's voice. It mirrored her own. However, Faith resolved to prepare herself for what might occur when Janay was released. At the same time, she cared about Evan and didn't want to abandon him. She thought about her options for a few moments and realized she couldn't turn her back on them. Not yet. Besides, her heart wasn't completely ready to walk away.

"I'll do my job. But no more spending the night, hanging out on the weekends and movie nights for you and me until you and Janay figure out what you're doing."

"That's fair. I need you, Faith. I want you to know that."

"You need me or you want me?"

After a brief hesitation Evan said, "Probably a little of both."

"You just remember that when your wife comes home. That's when I'll know how you really feel." Faith disconnected the call and decided to exercise a little self-care. Her bathtub, candles and e-reader had been calling her for weeks, but the Ingrams had taken precedence. Tonight, she would begin reversing that trend. Faith vowed to never forget her own needs again, regardless of what happened between her and Evan.

Chapter 31

Frank lifted his head from the back of the sofa. He wiped the sleep from his eyes and looked around his living room to clear his head. It was dark outside. The last thing he remembered was sitting on the couch trying to resolve his dilemma. He must've fallen asleep shortly after that.

He thought about all that had transpired. He was distressed about Janay leaving. She was his wife and he couldn't do without her love. He had to figure out how to get her back home. He figured that shouldn't be too hard because of the love they shared.

He would get revenge on Vonne since her lying convinced Janay to leave. Punishing Vonne's brats, Deasia and Trey, was next on his agenda. They had blatantly disobeyed him and started the chain of events that led to Janay leaving. When he got through with them, they wouldn't even think about doing that again. Now that he had a plan, he would begin carrying it out as soon as possible.

Frank detected movement outside the front window. A shadow passed by the window next to the couch he was sitting on, and then someone knocked on the door. A smile crept on his face.

"I knew you'd come back to me," he said heading for the door. Before he could open it, he heard someone speaking. He peeked out the window and saw police cars lining the street.

Frank picked up his cell phone and went into the basement. He quickly found the number he was searching for and pressed the call button.

"Before you say a word, let me tell you something. I don't appreciate you pointing that gun at me. In fact, I'm not even sure I want to hear what you have to say. So, if you're calling to threaten me again, we can just hang up now."

"Will you shut up and listen?" Frank whispered.

"Why are you whispering?" Vonne asked her brother.

"I guess you're happy now. The police are here."

"I did not call the police."

"Why are they here? I didn't do anything wrong."

"Frank, you kidnapped a woman and held her against her wishes. That's against the law, so you need to prepare to face the consequences. I know a lawyer. I'll give her a call. Let me see if I can get my neighbor to watch Deasia and Trey and I'll be right there."

"I can't afford a lawyer."

"You can't afford not to have a lawyer. I'll see you in a few minutes, Frank."

"No, don't come. It's not worth it."

"I'm not going to let you go through this alone. I'm on my way."

"You've helped me enough, Vonne. My wife is gone because of you. Stay there with your kids. I don't need your help. I got this."

***

Vonne pressed on the accelerator as she drove to her brother's home. She didn't care what Frank said. She sensed she needed to get there quickly since Frank seemed oblivious to the seriousness of the situation. She hoped she could reason with him. Perhaps, she could save him some trouble. As Vonne neared her brother's home, she noticed a barricade across the road to Frank's house. She pulled up to the officer at the barricade and lowered her window.

"I'm here to speak with my brother. He lives on the next block. Can I get through?"

"Ma'am, we have a police situation here and we're trying to restrict movement in the area until it's resolved."

"I really need to get to my brother. His name is Frank Scott. He called me a little while ago saying there were police at his home."

"Hold on a minute." The officer walked away.

After a brief conversation on his radio, he approached Vonne's vehicle once more.

"What's your name, ma'am?"

"I'm Vonne Scott."

116

The officer repeated this information to the person he was talking to.

"Park your car right here, ma'am. Someone is coming to escort you to the command center. Apparently, your brother mentioned you and they were trying to contact you." Vonne looked at her cell phone...dead. She hoped Frank hadn't tried to call her back. She wanted him to know she was there to support him through this.

Another officer approached the barricade as Vonne sat in her car. The first officer waved her over. She hoped she could rescue her brother from himself.

Vonne arrived at the mobile command center, surprised by all the activity. It seemed like a lot to deal with one man. She didn't know the details of what Frank had done, but it had to be major based on what she was seeing.

An officer pressed a cell phone into her hands. "He won't talk to anyone but you. See if you can talk him into ending this standoff."

"Frank, this is Vonne. I'm outside. The police said they've been trying to get you to come out. I don't want you to get hurt. Frank...please... Just come out and end this."

"I want them to go away and leave me alone. I didn't do anything wrong."

"There is no other way for you to make it out of this. These people are not playing with you. They have the street blocked off and there are police all over the place. I don't even want to think about what might happen if you don't surrender."

"Death doesn't scare me. I've been dying on the inside ever since Mama did what she did to me. I don't see a need to let these people treat me any kind of way, too."

"I know you haven't gotten over Mama giving you away, but this isn't the way to handle it."

"Daddy left because he hated me. Then, Mama got mad because I made him leave. Even my foster parents didn't want me. If that many people feel that way about you, you know you must be bad. How do you think that makes me feel?"

"None of that is true. Mama and Daddy had their own problems with each other. It didn't have anything to do with you."

"I don't even know why I'm talking to you about this. I don't expect you to understand. You were never a foster kid. Why didn't they give you away?"

"Frank. You had some great foster parents. Remember Miss Zee? She loved you. She took great care of you, didn't she?"

Frank chuckled so hard it turned into full-fledged laughter. "She was the worst foster parent ever. She just wanted me to do nasty things with her."

"Well, I love you and so do Deasia and Trey. We're going to get through this together. But, you have to come out. This isn't making things any better. I'm begging you."

"All I ever wanted was to love someone and for someone to love me. Is that too much to ask? Janay is the only one and now she's gone." Vonne's heart broke as she listened to her brother crying on the other end of the line.

"Please, Frank."

"Maybe it's time for me to leave here. Maybe God will love me. I heard somewhere He is love."

"Don't talk like that. God does love you, Frank. But, you don't have to go anywhere to find love."

"No, I think it's time. I don't think I have any more chances at love. I think I'd rather die."

"Frank. No," Vonne cried.

"I'm coming out," Frank said then disconnected the call.

"Dispatch, we have a door open," an officer declared.

"He's got a gun. Drop the gun!"

Vonne shot out of the unit and sprinted toward Frank's house. She hadn't gotten far before the police stopped her. She was close enough to see her brother standing in a flood of light with a huge smile on his face.

The officer began pulling Vonne away from the scene. "Ma'am, it's not safe for you to be this close. We don't want you to get hurt."

"Please don't shoot him. He really is harmless."

"We have to stop the threat. If he disarms himself, we won't have to do that."

"Drop the weapon!"

Vonne glanced over her shoulder. She could see Frank lifting a rifle close to the side of his face. Suddenly, she heard shots ring out.

"Oh, my God! No!" Vonne fell to her knees knowing instinctively that her brother was gone, never feeling the love he so desperately desired.

Chapter 32

"Ouch! You braid too tight." Janay flinched and pulled her head away from her sister.

Cherlynn lifted her hands from her sister's head. "Will you let me finish? I only have one more cornrow and I'll be done. If you would tie your hair up at night, I wouldn't have to keep fixing these braids every time I come see you."

"It feels like you're braiding my brain. Promise me you'll lighten up a little. Otherwise, I'll just have to deal with it the way it is."

"There is no way I'm going to leave you looking like this. I promise I won't make it as tight."

Big Momma chuckled. "You always were tender headed. You used to give me the same kind of fits when you were little."

"Hey, everyone," Evan said as he entered the room. He hugged Big Momma and Cherlynn who responded to his greeting.

He turned his attention to Janay. "How are you today?" He kissed her on the forehead.

"Feeling pretty good."

"I'm glad to hear it." Evan lifted a colorful duffle bag onto Janay's lap. "I brought you some things."

She opened the bag and pulled out her tablet, mp3 player, Bible, a few framed photos and other personal items.

Looking at the photos brought tears to Janay's eyes. "Aww, look at them. My babies have grown so much. I can't wait to see them. Where are they, anyway?"

"They're with Faith." Evan shifted in his seat.

"These are such good pictures. Which one of you did their hair? I know Evan didn't do it. And where did these dresses come from? They're gorgeous." Janay continued shuffling through the pictures.

"Um, Faith is responsible for all of that." Evan, Big Momma and Cherlynn exchanged glances.

"I'll have to thank her when I see her." Janay looked back and forth between her loved ones. "What?"

Big Momma stood and motioned for Cherlynn to do the same. "Honey, we're going to get out of here so you and Evan can spend some time together." She and Cherlynn hugged Janay.

Big Momma turned toward Evan and mouthed, "Tell her." She and Cherlynn hugged Evan, then left.

"Tell me what? What is she talking about?"

Evan clasped his hands in his lap. "All you need to be concerned about right now is getting better."

"You know I'm going to worry if you don't tell me."

"Okay, look. It's no big deal, but I'll tell you."

"I'm listening."

"While you were gone, I needed a lot of help. Big Momma and Cherlynn did what they could but the girls and I needed a little more support."

Janay nodded. "Okay."

"Faith became more involved in our day-to-day life. In the process, she and I became friends. Big Momma and Cherlynn didn't think that was a good idea."

"Why would they have a problem with you and Faith being friends?"

"They think we got a little too close."

Janay picked imaginary lint from her bedding. "How close did you get?" She returned her gaze to Evan.

"She spends a little more time with us than she did before. She does movie nights and fun nights with us. That's all. It's nothing to worry about. Trust me."

"Movie nights and fun nights? She shuts down at six in the evening."

"I told you she did a little extra while you were gone."

Janay squinted. "Is there more to the story than you're telling me?"

Evan looked away. "There's nothing else to tell."

Janay noticed Evan's unwillingness to meet her eyes. "Did you and Faith become involved or something?"

Evan didn't speak for what seemed like several moments.

Janay's mouth fell open. "Oh, my goodness! You're having an affair with Faith!" Janay took a slipper from her bag and threw it at Evan who ducked. "How long has this been going on?"

Evan stood. He reached to embrace Janay. "Calm down. There is no affair."

Janay pushed him away. "Then what do you call it?"

Evan managed to place his hand over Janay's. "We're friends. That's it." Janay pulled her hand from Evan's.

"Mrs. Ingram, is everything okay?" A nurse asked, peeking his head into the room. "We heard you raising your voice."

Janay didn't respond. Instead, she sat breathing heavily; her arms folded and tears flowing.

"Mr. Ingram, I'm going to have to ask you to leave. You seem to be upsetting your wife."

"But, I don't want to leave."

"Please, just give her some time to settle down. You can come back tomorrow."

"Do you want me to leave?" Evan asked Janay.

Janay rolled her eyes but didn't say a word.

Evan leaned over to hug her. She turned away from him. "I love you." He kissed the back of her head and left.

The nurse checked Janay's vitals. "Is there anything I can get for you?"

"Yes, I need to get out of here. When will I be discharged?"

"I don't know, Mrs. Ingram. I can ask."

"Please do. I need to get home."

Chapter 33

"I can't believe you signed yourself out of the hospital against the doctor's recommendation," Cherlynn said as she wheeled her car onto her sister's street.

Janay turned toward her sister. "I can't believe you knew my husband had something going on with the babysitter and didn't tell me."

"What was I going to say? I don't know what's going on between them."

"That's okay. I'll see for myself."

"I really don't think this is a good idea," Cherlynn told Janay as her car came to a stop in Evan and Janay's driveway.

"I know. You've been telling me that over and over again since you picked me up."

"Big Momma is waiting for you. She's going to be so disappointed when I come home without you. Why don't we just go there and I'll bring you back here later?"

"No, I've been away long enough."

"Are you sure you're going to be okay?" Cherlynn tilted her head toward the car in the driveway.

"I'm sure." Janay eyed the familiar car sitting in the driveway. "I need to handle this and I need to do it alone. Don't worry. I'll be okay."

Both women stepped out of the car. Cherlynn grabbed Janay's bag from the backseat and walked around the car to her little sister.

Cherlynn hugged Janay. "Look, I'm just a phone call away. Call me if you need anything."

Janay took the bag. "I will, sis. You go on home and I'll call later."

Cherlynn got back in the car. Janay faced her home. She'd been told six months had passed since she last left this house. She walked up the stairs to the porch and realized she had no idea where her keys were. She clearly didn't think this through. She rang the doorbell and heard footsteps on the other side of the door. The door opened and Janay found herself face-to-face with the woman who kept her place warm while she was away.

Faith didn't seem surprised to see her, though Janay thought she should be. Janay wondered what she was doing opening the door to the home where *her* husband and *her* children live. The two women stared at each other for several minutes as if attempting to memorize every hair, pore and blemish on the other woman's face. Faith pulled the door open further and stepped aside allowing her easy passage into her home. Her home. She didn't want to respond to Faith's welcoming gesture because to do so would mean it was hers to give and it wasn't. She had stolen it. Janay entered and looked around. Her furniture had been rearranged. One of the living room walls was painted a different color. And now a different woman stood cooking in the kitchen. Janay sniffed the air. This wasn't an ordinary meal either. It smelled fancy. Important. Like it had significance. It was prepared with love. Janay's stomach growled, indicating its agreement with her assessment. It sounded like a bear in heat.

Janay returned her attention to Faith. "You can leave now," she declared as her way of dismissing this trespasser from their lives.

"I can't," Faith said simply as if those words resolved the issue.

"You walked in here didn't you?"

"I did."

"Then, if you leave now, it shouldn't be too difficult for you to walk yourself up out of here. Now, if you stay much longer, that might not be the case."

"I'm in too deep."

"Sounds like a personal problem to me."

"It is," Faith admitted.

"I know you've been playing wife in my absence, but I'm back now. You are no longer wanted or needed here."

"That's not what Evan says."

"Oh really. I'm sure you misunderstood him. What purpose could you possibly serve now? I don't even think I want you babysitting the Ns anymore."

Faith's breath caught in her throat, but she quickly recovered. "I think you should ask your husband about my purpose."

Janay's stomach growled even louder, as if the two women in the room didn't hear it the first time. *Obviously, my stomach thinks her purpose is to feed me*, Janay thought.

Ignoring her rumbling stomach, she propped her hand on her hip and rolled her neck. "Why don't you tell me?"

Faith didn't respond. Janay glared at her. *Unbelievable*, she thought. She detected something in Faith's eyes, her stance... even her body language.

"You're in love with my husband. Aren't you?"

Faith didn't speak, but Janay's stomach did.

"Oh, my goodness. You can't think he feels the same way. Do you?"

"It doesn't matter what I think."

"Are you sleeping with Evan?"

"Absolutely not."

Faith peered into Janay's eyes for a few seconds, so the woman could see the truth in her response.

"I'll be leaving now," Faith declared. "Tell Evan I'll talk with him later."

"Um, mmm. No, you won't be doing that. Please leave your key on the table on your way out."

"I'll give it to Evan if he asks for it."

Janay approached Faith slowly, stopping just short of bumping toes. "Obviously you're a little confused. This is my house and you will give me the key."

Faith moved closer to Janay and threatened the tops of her toes. "I'm not confused at all. I didn't get the key from you, so I'm not returning it to you."

"I don't know what went on while I was gone to make you so confident here in my house. But, rest assured, you will be put in your place very soon."

"Or maybe you'll be put in yours." Faith snatched her purse from the counter and walked toward the door. She stopped suddenly, with her back to Janay. "A couple of things before I go, Naomi's taking a nap. I heard your stomach growling. There's seafood lasagna in the oven. Help yourself. It's ready." Then she left for what Janay hoped would be the last time.

Janay walked into the kitchen and pulled the glass dish holding the seafood lasagna, another woman had lovingly prepared for her family, out of the oven. It looked as delectable as it smelled. She was trying to figure out what do with it when her body cast its vote. She went to the cabinet and found glasses where the plates used to be. She continued opening cabinets until she finally found what she was looking for. She snatched a plate from the stack and scooped a portion of the lasagna onto it, placing a forkful in her mouth. It. Was. Scrumptious.

Once again her thoughts turned toward the glass dish. For a moment, she thought about passing it off to her family as something she prepared. Then, she realized they would never believe it because this wasn't the type of meal she would cook. It would be a shame to waste the lobster, crab and shrimp, but she made a decision in that moment. Janay decided to throw the rest of it out just like she threw Faith out. She scooped another portion onto her plate, turned on the water and the garbage disposal, picked the dish up and turned it upside down over the sink. Janay watched as the cheese, noodles, sauce and seafood found their way down the drain.

She looked at the clock and realized she had time to cook something else for her family and began searching through the cabinets and refrigerator to see what she had to work with. Janay decided to cook some of her specialties - fried chicken, macaroni and cheese, black-eyed peas and a few other things if time allowed. She would replace memories of Faith just like she was replacing her meal. Janay kicked off her shoes and jacket and got to work.

**

"Call Evan," Faith directed her phone as she left the Ingram home with tears traveling down her face. She attempted to remove her emotions from her voice before he answered. She wanted him to take her seriously and knew if there were tears involved, he would just pass it off as her being emotional. The phone rang a few times before his administrative assistant answered.

"Hello. Evan Ingram's office. How may I assist you?"

"Hi, Olivia. This is Faith. Is Evan available?"

"Hi, Faith. He's in a meeting right now. Is there a message?"

"I really need to speak with him. I promise I won't hold him long." Faith's voice cracked. She felt herself begin to hyperventilate. Olivia must have heard it because, without a word, she got Evan to the phone.

"Faith? Is everything okay? Olivia said you sounded like something was wrong."

"I was at your house cooking dinner and Janay came she tried to put me out Evan she told me I couldn't babysit the girls anymore and I couldn't talk to you anymore you're going to have to talk to her and let her know what's going on," she blurted out with no breath between words.

"Janay was at the house?"

"Yes, I answered the door and let her in."

"I didn't know she was getting out today."

"Well, she did, Evan. And now, I don't know what's going to happen because she definitely wants you back and I don't know how we're going to handle this." Faith inhaled and exhaled slowly, trying to regain control of her breathing.

"Calm down. Can we meet at the Batchelor's Bayou Café when I get off?" Faith was silent as she contemplated the meaning behind his response.

"Batchelor's Bayou Café?"

"Yes."

"Sooo, we're hiding now?"

"Obviously, we can't go to my house."

"What are you saying, Evan?"

"I really don't know what I'm saying. I'm confused."

"You weren't confused while I was cooking and cleaning and putting my life on hold for you and the girls. You were clear then."

"It's different now. Janay is home."

"You mean the wife you're planning to divorce?"

Evan hesitated a moment before speaking. Things were happening quicker than he was ready for. He hadn't even been able to process his own feelings. Now, he was faced with dealing with Faith and he didn't know how.

"Faith, I'm sorry."

"So Janay was right. I have served my purpose."

"I don't know what to say. I wish things were different."

"Yeah, me too," Faith said prior to disconnecting the call. She threw her phone onto the passenger seat and pounded the steering wheel with her hands. *How did I get myself into this? I knew better but I chose to follow my heart and look what it got me.*

Chapter 34

"I'm coming," Macie yelled, approaching the front door of her condominium. The banging continued as she pulled back the curtains in her living room to get a peek at who was demanding entry. She unlocked the door and opened it. Looking at Faith, she knew something was wrong.

"Are you gonna let me in?" Faith asked pulling on the handle of the locked screen door.

"Is somebody chasing you?"

"What makes you think someone's chasing me?"

"The way you're banging on my door, somebody must be after you and I don't want them in here," Macie said with her arms folded across her chest.

"Would I be standing here talking to you this calmly if that was the case?"

"You got a point. Come on in," Macie pushed open the screen door allowing Faith to enter.

Faith plopped herself onto Macie's couch. "Aren't you going to ask me what's going on?"

"I will in a minute. I just made some fresh strawberry lemonade. Want some?"

"That would be awesome. I'll take a few strawberries on the side, too."

Five minutes later Macie returned to the room with a tray holding a pitcher, two stemmed glasses and a bowl of strawberries. She sat in the chair adjacent to the couch and filled their glasses.

"What's going on, girl?"

"Janay came home today and I don't know where that leaves me."

"I told you not to get involved with that woman's husband. But no, you didn't listen," Macie said.

"I don't know how it happened. I was just helping with the girls and the next thing I knew I was falling in love with the man." Faith closed her eyes and dropped her head on the back of the couch.

"You don't know? Let me tell you. You spent way too much time with him when you should've stayed in the babysitter lane. You were spending the night over there, cooking meals, doing family fun nights..." Macie jerked her head toward her friend. "You didn't...you know...did you?"

"We never allowed things to go there. He is a married man, you know?"

"Yeah, I did know and so did you. But that didn't stop you from falling in love with him, now did it?"

"What am I going to do?" Faith questioned her friend as tears streamed down her face.

Macie sat on the sofa next to Faith and offered her a tissue. "You're going to move on."

"What do you mean move on?"

"You're a single woman. Act like it. Evan and the Ns are Janay's responsibility. Not yours."

"I got myself into a mess, didn't I?" Faith dropped her head into her hands.

"You did, but you can get out."

Faith lifted her head quickly, eyes wide with hope and wiped her tears. "Maybe he'll still choose me. I mean, after all, he was going to divorce Janay."

"Faith, honey, now that he knows she didn't abandon their family, I'm sure that changes things."

"You don't understand. I can't just walk away."

"You have to."

"I don't know that for sure."

"I think you do, dear."

"Maybe he's just confused right now. You know, surprised that his wife is back. As soon as he remembers she didn't want him anymore, he'll come to his senses," Faith said as she scooted to the edge of the couch.

Macie shifted to the cocktail table. Sitting directly in front of her friend, she grabbed her firmly by her shoulders, "Faith, whether he's confused about his marriage or not, he is still married. Back away."

"Not until he tells me it's over for sure." Faith dried her face with her hands.

"All right, I'm trying to help you, but you're intent on bumping your head. Don't worry, though. I'll be here to bandage you up when you get another emotional boo-boo."

"Keep the emotional Band-Aid on standby. If I do this right, I won't need it," Faith said as she left Macie's house with renewed hope that things might still work out in her favor.

Chapter 35

Evan pulled into the garage and said a brief prayer. He wasn't sure what kind of mood Janay was in considering how upset Faith was. He didn't know what they had discussed, but he was sure it wasn't too friendly. Once Faith hung up on him, he decided to go home and check on Janay. Since his wife's reappearance, the focus had been on her emotional and physical well-being. Now, they needed to start the process of determining the future of their marriage.

He walked into the house and immediately noticed the aroma of food. He found Janay in the kitchen frosting a cake. Fried chicken, macaroni and cheese, green beans with potatoes and something else in a covered dish were on display on the kitchen counter.

"Hi, Evan," Janay said smiling. She awkwardly hugged her husband who stood stiff as a statue.

"Hi. Umm, why didn't you tell me you were getting out today? I would've picked you up."

"I wanted to surprise you. But, the surprise was on me when I found Faith here."

"She was a big help around here while you were gone."

"Umm hmm, you told me that. What you didn't tell me about was all these feelings."

"We can talk about that later."

"Why don't we talk about it now?"

"Let's just have a nice family dinner and we'll talk later tonight if you're still here."

"Why wouldn't I be here?"

"The last I knew you were unhappy and wanted a separation. I don't know if you want to be here or not."

Janay dropped her head, "I guess I did say that."

"Yes, you did. So, is that still what you want?"

"Maybe we should talk a little later. This discussion might take a while."

Evan turned away from Janay and started up the stairs. "I'm going to pick up the girls from school."

"I should probably get Naomi up. I don't want her to be up all night."

"I'll get her up and take her with me," Evan said, holding his arm out to halt Janay's movement.

"Why can't she stay here?"

"This is the new routine."

"Well, I'll come with you. I can't wait to see Nahla and Nia. I've missed them so much."

"Not today," Evan responded as he disappeared onto the home's upper level.

"What just happened?" Janay whispered as she stood at the bottom of the stairs. She had expected her and Evan's reunion to be more celebratory. Instead, it felt awkward. She felt like...the other woman.

***

Evan pushed the stroller carrying a still-dozing Naomi onto the school grounds. The sun was shining and the weather warm. It was the perfect day to walk and clear his head. He looked at his watch and realized the girls wouldn't be released for another ten minutes. He had arrived a bit early in his haste to remove himself from Janay's presence.

"Hi, Evan," a voice spoke behind him. He turned, shading his eyes from the sun. Staring into her eyes, he saw questions begging for answers and hurt that existed because she had to ask them. He regretted putting them there.

"Hi. What are you doing here?"

"This is what I do every day. I didn't know if Janay would think to pick the girls up or not," Faith said as she peeked at Naomi. She stroked the toddler's head and face lightly. Naomi awakened with a whimper.

"I'm here, so you don't have to stay." Evan unfastened Naomi from her stroller and picked her up. Her eyes landed on Faith and she reached out for her. Faith obliged her by taking the toddler in her arms. Naomi's whimpering stopped immediately.

"I don't mind staying if it means I can spend a few moments with you and Naomi."

"Faith…" Evan hesitated looking down at the ground, "Truthfully, I'd rather be alone with my thoughts right now. I hope you understand." He looked back at Faith.

"I won't say a word. I just need to feel your presence."

The school doors flew open and the schoolyard was flooded with children. Nia and Nahla walked out of the building holding hands. They looked around until they saw Evan, Faith and Naomi and ran toward them.

Faith greeted the girls and drew them close with her free arm.

"Hi girls. Are you ready to go home? There's a surprise there for you," Evan greeted his daughters.

"Yay, we like surprises," Nahla cheered, jumping up and down. "Do you know what the surprise is, Miss Faith?"

"Maybe. But, I won't spoil it for you," Faith said with a wink.

"Let's go. I want to see what it is," Nahla grabbed Faith's hand.

"Um, honey, Miss Faith isn't going to our house today."

"Aww, but we want her to come. It's no fun without her," Nahla pleaded.

"I beg your pardon? I am the fun master," Evan said, feigning offense.

"It's different, Daddy. Faith is a girl. She understands girl stuff," Nahla smiled at her dad.

"Oh, I see. We've got to get going. Tell Miss Faith goodbye so you can see the surprise."

Nahla studied Faith's face for a moment. "Are you okay, Miss Faith? You don't look happy."

"I'm fine. Give me a hug so you can go see your surprise." Nia and Nahla hugged Faith as Evan took Naomi from her arms and placed her back in the stroller.

Faith hugged Evan and whispered, "I'm not giving up on us. I hope you won't either." She released him and headed for her car

Nahla watched Faith until she disappeared into her vehicle. "She needs us to pray for her, Daddy. Something isn't right. Miss Faith seems so sad. When we say our prayers tonight, can we pray for her?"

"Yes, baby and maybe you can pray for Daddy, too."

"I always do."

Chapter 36

Feeling crushed by the weight of his concerns, Evan changed into his pajamas and went to brush his teeth. He looked at his reflection in the mirror. The wrinkles on his forehead and the noticeable frown lines revealed the effects of the happenings of the past months and the weight of the decision he needed to make. He went into the bedroom where he paced the floor next to the king size bed he and Janay shared. He loved her. When she disappeared, it devastated him. Yet, he had found solace in Faith's presence. He wanted to move on from Janay and develop a love relationship with Faith.

But, he still loved Janay. Even more so once he found out why she disappeared and what she had experienced. How could he hurt either one of these women? How could he choose?

Evan needed to take his concerns to God and ask for His guidance. He lowered himself to his knees. As he did, Janay entered the room.

"Do you mind if I pray with you?" She asked approaching Evan.

"Sure," Evan replied.

After their prayer, Evan sat on the side of the bed while Janay headed to the other side. She removed her robe and Evan noticed the low back on the gown she was wearing. He wanted to touch her; hold her; love her. He walked around to her side of the bed and reached out to touch her face. She jumped. It was only her first night home. What did he expect? A vision of Faith in that sexy nightgown ran through his mind. Not wanting to complicate an already complicated situation, he grabbed his pillow. "I'm going to sleep in the guest room."

"Why?" Janay asked softly.

"I think it's best for now."

"Please stay. I need to feel some sort of normalcy."

Evan shook his head. "Good night, Janay. Get some rest. I'll see you in the morning."

As Evan settled into the bed in the guest room, he caught a whiff of a fragrance and realized it belonged to Faith. He smiled as he closed his eyes and snuggled under the covers, relishing in the comfort the scent provided. Moments later, Janay's sobs interrupted the silence and destroyed the joy his retreat provided.

***

Faith tossed and turned from one side of her bed to the other. She looked at the clock on her cell phone. For the past few hours, the day's events played over and over in her mind like a bad movie. The moment she laid eyes on Janay that afternoon, she knew there would be trouble. Although angered by the level of disrespect Janay showed, Evan's dismissal disturbed her more.

How could Evan discard her after everything she sacrificed for the family? Just because Janay returned didn't give him the right to kick her out of their lives. She had loved and cared for them and she thought Evan felt the same way about her. Knowing Evan didn't caused her heart to ache. They were an integral part of each other's lives. Now, she didn't know where she stood. *I wonder if Janay stayed there tonight. Are they reconciling? Are they making love? Am I still the babysitter? Am I forgotten?* Faith continued to toss and turn. *God, please give me peace and allow me sweet sleep.*

Chapter 37

The following morning the family gathered for breakfast. Janay got up early and prepared bacon, eggs, hash browns, pancakes and fresh-squeezed orange juice.

"Why don't you say grace, Janay?" Evan said as he laid his napkin in his lap.

"I think you should say it, Evan." Janay responded.

Nahla looked from her mother to her father. "I'll say grace," she said, closing her eyes and bowing her head.

"Go ahead, baby," Janay encouraged.

"God, thank you for this food we are about to eat. Thank you for Mommy coming home like I asked. Thank you for Daddy being here to take care of us while Mommy was gone. Thank you for Miss Faith who takes good care of us, too. Amen."

"Amen," the family spoke in agreement. Janay and Evan's eyes met as Janay rolled hers.

"Where's Miss Faith? Is she still sleep?" Nahla asked.

"Faith spends the night here?" Janay asked.

"Sometimes," Nahla explained.

"Really," Janay responded.

"What time is she coming? Saturday is fun day," Nahla asked.

"I don't know when Miss Faith will be back," Evan said stealing a glance at Janay.

"She has to be here Monday when we go to school."

"I was thinking. Wouldn't it be nice if I took you to school and picked you up every day? Just like before…" Janay asked keeping her gaze on Evan.

Nahla cheered and Nia imitated her. "Yay! Miss Faith will be here, too. We're going to have so much fun. Right, Mommy?"

Janay jabbed her fork into her pancakes. "I don't think so."

***

After breakfast, the girls went upstairs to make their beds as Evan and Janay cleaned the kitchen.

"I can't believe you had that woman in here being my kids' mother. This is all your fault," Janay spat as she moved around the kitchen slamming dishes in the sink and throwing other items around.

"She wasn't trying to be their mother. They were already close to her. You can't blame me for that."

"Now my daughters are asking for your make-believe wife and we both know they can never see her again."

"Why should they have to adjust to a new person because you're angry they're so attached to Faith?"

"Is this really about the Ns or you?"

145

Evan dropped his head and stuffed his hands in his pocket. "I don't know."

Janay pointed a fork at her husband. "Listen, I want you to hear me clearly. It's one thing for you to get caught up with Faith while I was away. It's another thing for you to still want her now that I'm home. I won't be the other woman in my own marriage. When you decide what you want, let me know. You don't have forever, though. So, keep that in mind." Janay swung around and stopped when she noticed her precious daughters Nahla and Nia standing at the top of the stairs. Nahla had tears trekking down her face and Nia appeared close to tears.

Concerned by their expression, Janay asked, "What's wrong, Honey Bear?"

"We heard you say we can't see Miss Faith anymore."

"Oh, don't worry. It's all going to work out just fine."

"Not if we can't see Miss Faith. We love her. We like it when we're with her. While you were looking for your happiness, she took good care of us."

Evan moved around Janay and stood at to the foot of the stairs. "I don't want you girls to worry. The grown-ups are going to get this whole thing figured out."

Nahla wiped her tears.

"Hey, I have an idea. Let's go to the park. Would you like that?" Evan asked.

"Yeah," Nahla and Nia yelled.

"Then can we get ice cream like we always do?" Nia asked.

"We sure can. But no more worrying, okay? We got a deal?" Evan pointed at his daughters.

"Yes, Daddy. Can we go now?"

"As soon as we get ready, we can."

Nahla and Nia took off toward their bedroom. Janay stormed up the stairs behind them leaving Evan to complete the cleanup.

Chapter 38

"Come on in and have a seat, Brother Ingram." Pastor Willis smiled as he came around his desk to greet Evan.

"Thanks, Pastor Willis," Evan shook the older man's hand and sat in a chair in front of his desk.

"How's Janay?" Pastor Willis asked while taking his seat.

"She's improving a little every day."

"That was such a terrible thing that happened to her. I'm praying for her," Pastor Willis folded his arms across his belly. "So, what brings you here?"

"Pastor... Janay and I are not in a good place right now. We're having difficulty reconnecting and I'm really concerned."

"Well, what Janay has been through tends to change a person. Adjusting is going to take some time." Pastor Willis said, leaning forward and repositioning his hands together on the desk.

"I agree with you on that. But...this has more to do with my feelings."

"Go on."

"I'm angry and I'm bitter. When Janay disappeared, I thought she had abandoned me and the girls."

"What made you think that?"

"Before she left, she told me she needed some time away from the family. I took that to mean she didn't want the marriage and family anymore. So, when she didn't come home from work that day, I thought that's what happened," Evan explained. "Over time, I became angry and resentful toward Janay. Even though I now know that wasn't why she left, I'm still ticked off that she even considered leaving us in the first place."

"I noticed a woman coming to church with you and the girls. Tell me, does she have anything to do with this?"

"You're talking about Faith, my daughters' babysitter. I think I've fallen in love with her."

"Hmm."

"At first Faith was just helping with the girls, but we developed feelings for each other. With Janay coming back, I'm confused. I don't want anyone to get hurt but no matter who I choose, the other person is going to be hurt."

"Son, first of all, you're going to have to attempt to reconcile with Janay. I know you're hurt about her desire for a separation. But, you're going to have to figure out how to let that go if you're going to stay together. The other thing is you must release Faith. If you don't, she'll be a distraction while you're trying to repair your marriage. It's unfair to expect her to wait. I'm not going to say it will be easy. But, if the two of you commit to this marriage, I believe it can survive."

"But, I don't want to let Faith go."

"You can't have it both ways. As your pastor, I have to remind you of your vows and your responsibility to live accordingly. You prematurely emotionally divorced your wife and started a relationship with Faith. That goes against the promises you made before God. Let's pray."

Chapter 39

Evan entered her home. Faith immediately noticed his slumped shoulders, concerned facial expression and lack of eye contact. She sensed what he was there to tell her would not be in her favor. She thought her relationship with Evan was solid, especially after Janay had been gone for so long. Now, Faith was afraid Janay's return would prove otherwise. She braced herself for what she was sure was coming.

"Hi, Evan," Faith said as Evan silently walked passed her. She closed the door behind him and waited to hear what he had to say.

He took one hand out of his pocket, waved then stuck it back into its hiding place. His eyes only momentarily left the floor as he stood in the middle of her living room.

"Would you like to sit down?" She offered.

"Sure," he responded, crossing the small room to sit on the loveseat while she sat in a chair.

"It's good to see you. You look good." *Why am I lying to him? He looks like he hasn't rested in quite some time.*

"Thanks," Evan replied absently.

"How are the girls?" She asked, trying to fill the silence.

"They're okay. They've been asking for you," Evan glanced at her, his face devoid of a smile or pleasant facial expression.

"I'd love to see them."

"You know that's not possible right now."

"That doesn't stop me from missing them or wanting to see them."

Silence fell between them. Faith wasn't sure she wanted to break it. To do so might not be in her best interest emotionally. After a few more awkward moments, she decided it would be better to hear the truth than to sit there guessing.

"So, what brings you here?"

"How've you been?" Evan asked.

"About the same as you," she told him, letting him know they were in the same boat. Their eyes briefly connected before his returned to the floor.

"I came to talk about us."

"Okay." Faith sat back in the chair, prepared to listen.

"When Janay left I was shocked and didn't know what to do. Your support was a Godsend."

"I'm glad I could help."

"I was so vulnerable, Faith. I never should've let you get so close. I wasn't ready for what you wanted."

"Say what now?" Faith asked with an attitude.

"I couldn't resist you. I was powerless against you."

"Hold on. Are you trying to say I took advantage of you?"

"I'm not sure," he stated, holding eye contact for a moment.

"Well, let me assure you. I did not. As a matter of fact, I think it was the other way around. You took advantage of me." Faith rose from her seat, folded her arms and paced the floor.

"How?"

"I did everything a wife and mother would do, you know? Except for sex."

"Maybe that was part of your plan," Evan stated, unaware of the look she shot him because his eyes avoided hers.

"Part of my plan? Somebody fell and bumped their head. Hard."

"You're a single woman who's never been married. You saw me and my Ns as an opportunity for a ready-made family."

"What? I tried to put some distance between us, but you wouldn't allow it. And what about that night in the hall?" She questioned.

"By that time, I was already falling in love with you."

"Oh, so I guess I made that happen too."

Evan stood, deep in thought.

"Yes. You did."

"Did I make Janay leave? Did I make you hunt her down so you could get a divorce? Did I do all of that, too?"

Evan looked as though he hadn't taken those facts into account.

"Once again, why are you here?" She asked, losing her temper.

"I want my heart back," he stated with tears in his eyes and a sob in his throat. "I can't give it to Janay because you have it." He bent over with his face in his hands, bawling.

"Oh, I see. It's all becoming clear to me now." Faith launched a throw pillow at Evan. "You're here because you're feeling guilty that you don't love your wife anymore and you need someone to blame. I can't believe I ever fell in love with a man like you, Evan Ingram. You know good and well I didn't seduce you or trick you or take advantage of you. But, if that's what you need to think of me to feel better about yourself, then I'm sure you don't want to be in my company." Faith walked to the door and opened it. "Please leave."

"Wait, you love me?"

"Get out of my house. Now!" She yelled, insulted by the implication of his words.

He walked to the door, stopping to look back at her as though he was trying to memorize the essence of her very being, then he turned and left without another word. The man she loved. Faith wasn't sure he would ever return and didn't know if she wanted him to. She slammed the door shut with such force, the picture on the wall rattled.

Chapter 40

Evan sat across the table from Janay at Batchelor's Bayou Café. He thought the restaurant's brightly colored Mardi Gras-style décor might provide a more relaxed atmosphere for reconnecting. The hostess sat them in a booth on the far side of the restaurant.

"It seems like I haven't been here in years," Janay said surveying her surroundings. "This is one of my favorite spots."

Evan smiled; pleased he finally brought Janay some joy. He reached for her hands and looked into her eyes. "I knew you loved it here. That's why I chose it."

"Thank you. This is wonderful. I love you, baby."

"I love you too, honey." Evan lifted her hands to his mouth and kissed them, drawing a smile from Janay.

"I believe we're going to get through this, and we'll be even better than before."

"I agree. Better than ever." Evan felt hopeful about their marriage and reaffirmed his commitment to making the relationship work.

Janay picked up her menu and perused the selections. "Doggone it. They don't have the fried chicken salad on the menu anymore." She closed the menu, lifted it up above her head with both hands and slammed it down on the table. "I really had a taste for that."

"Calm down, honey. I'm sure you can find something else."

"I don't want anything else. I wanted that," she said pouting.

"Keep looking through the menu," Evan said as he placed the menu back in Janay's hands. "I'm sure you'll find something else that sounds good."

Evan peeked at his wife over his menu. Though the physical evidence of the ordeal had disappeared, the emotional and mental effects obviously lingered. Janay would have never thrown a fit like that before the kidnapping.

"Oh, I can't even believe this," Janay said looking at the entrance.

Evan's eyes followed Janay's. He couldn't believe it either. Faith and Jamison entered the eatery.

Faith looked away after her eyes met Evan's. Jamison waved and Evan responded with a wave as well.

"Who is that man with Faith?" Janay asked nodding her head toward Faith and Jamison.

"That's Jamison Lewis, the private investigator I hired to find you."

"How does Faith know him?"

"They were engaged at some point, but I don't know what their status is now."

It bothered Evan to see Faith with Jamison. He couldn't stop himself from staring at their table. He knew he wasn't supposed to care, but he did.

"Since you can't stop looking over there, why don't we just go over and—"

"Okay." Evan jumped up and rushed to the table before Janay could get the words completely out of her mouth.

***

"It looks like your employers are on their way to our table," Jamison warned.

"No way," Faith said.

"Hi, Faith. Jamison," Evan said, waving his hand.

"Hello," Faith and Jamison said in concert.

Jamison stood and turned his attention to Janay. "Janay, right? I'm Jamison Lewis. How are you?" he asked, extending his hand to shake hers.

"Thanks for asking. I'm getting better every day."

"I'm glad you're safe. It's nice to finally meet you," Jamison responded, taking his seat.

While Jamison and Evan engaged in small talk, Janay noticed Evan's eyes stayed on Faith. Jealous that another woman held Evan's heart, she sneered at Faith like she wanted to end her existence and zap her to make her disappear. Janay's nose and mouth were upturned in a snarl as though someone at the table hadn't showered in weeks.

Faith thought she was already invisible to them. However, looking into Evan's eyes and reading Janay's body language, she knew that wasn't true. She was still a part of this family regardless of their attempts to erase her from the family portrait. Faith smirked as she remembered Janay saying she had served her purpose and would be put in her place.

"Evan, let's go. I'm not hungry anymore," Janay said after breaking her gaze.

"What's wrong? I thought you wanted to eat here," Evan questioned.

"I'd rather get some fast food," she said turning up her nose at Faith once again.

"Please...stay. Why don't you all join us?" Jamison invited.

"We'd love to," Evan said, moving to take a seat.

"No, thank you. Jamison, it was nice to meet you," Janay said as she headed for the door.

"I'm sorry. She's still adjusting. We'll get together some other time." Evan left the table and ran after her.

***

"Wow! She is mad at you." Jamison said.

"So, it seems," Faith responded.

"If it makes you feel better, Evan was upset when he found out about you and me."

"He was?"

"Yeah, he said I needed to back off because you weren't available."

"Really," Faith said glancing toward Evan and Janay through the window as they entered their car.

"He threatened to fire me when I told him I wouldn't stop pursuing you."

"You guys were fighting over me?"

"No, he was fighting over you. You were already my woman," Jamison said looking deeply into Faith's eyes.

"I see."

"Faith, do you still want a relationship with Evan? Even though he's clearly back with his wife."

"Just because they were having lunch with each other doesn't mean they're together. I mean, we're sitting here having a meal and that doesn't mean we're back together," Faith reasoned.

"You're right. We're not *back* together."

"Thank you."

"Because, in my mind, we were never apart."

***

The interior of the Ingram's car was cold and silent as Janay and Evan rode home, though the chill was from the tension inside not from the weather outside.

Watching Evan drown Faith in all that attention sickened Janay. Here Faith was with a perfectly good looking, single man who obviously adored her but Evan, who should be showering his wife with love, seemed to be competing for the "who loves Faith more" award. This was too much for Janay to handle.

Janay stared at Evan trying to figure out how to address Evan's obvious connection to Faith.

Evan noticed her staring. "What?" He asked.

"I'm trying to figure out if you're being dishonest with yourself or with me."

Evan responded, "What are you talking about?"

"I think you might be in love with her. You were jealous when you saw her with Jamison."

"Look, I'm not going to keep explaining this to you. If we're going to stay together, you can't keep bringing that up."

"Hmm, now it's my responsibility to ignore the obvious."

"I'm focused on us. Not Faith. Why are we talking about her?"

"We can say we're focused on our marriage all we want. But until you deal with that situation, we won't be able to work on our relationship."

Chapter 41

Janay's car came to rest in her mother's driveway. It was unclear how she ended up there. She had been driving around thinking about how to overcome the deficit in her marriage. Something on the inside of her must've known she needed to talk to her mother. There was no one else she could talk to about the fact her husband and children had developed a deep emotional bond with someone else. She spoke to a few of her closest friends who told her to pray for Evan and everything would be okay. Well, she'd been praying for everyone including herself and what had it gotten her? A broken marriage. Her children crying for Faith and a heart that couldn't take much more.

A knock on her window startled her, bringing her out of her thoughts. "Come on in. No use in you sitting out here," Big Momma yelled, motioning for her to enter the house.

Janay entered her childhood home and Big Momma hugged her. There was no other place that felt like this, surrounded by her mother's love. She fought to keep her tears from escaping as her mother led her to the kitchen table where a cup of tea awaited, as if she knew Janay was coming. Big Momma took a sip of coffee then motioned for Janay to sit at the table.

"How you doing?"

"I'm alright, Momma."

After a moment, Big Momma shook her head, "Something's not right. What is it?"

Janay inhaled deeply and exhaled her truth. "I'm tired of trying to decide whether I should keep fighting for my marriage. I'm tired of trying to stop the movie of what happened to me playing in my mind. This is all just too much. I feel like I'm losing it."

"You are not losing your mind. You just have more healing to do, honey," Big Momma rubbed the side of Janay's face. This gesture from her childhood caused the tears she'd kept under lock and key to flow. Sobs soon followed. "That's it. Let it all out."

Big Momma left the dining room, returning with a wet washcloth and a box of tissue. Another gesture from Janay's childhood.

Once she composed herself enough to speak, Janay shared her true struggle. "I was wrong for wanting a separation. I'll admit that. No one knows how much I wish I had handled that a different way. But, how much longer is God going to punish me for that one mistake?"

"Listen here. God is not punishing you."

"Well this whole kidnapping ordeal started right after I told Evan I was leaving. Then I come home and find out Evan replaced me with his make-believe wife. If that's not a punishment, I don't know what is."

Big Momma took another long sip of coffee and slowly placed her cup back on the table. "I understand why you might feel that way, but I still don't believe any of this was punishment. I do think there may be a bigger purpose behind all of this."

"You do?"

"Yes, I do. Somebody had to go through this so others know they can get through it, too. Your story is going to be just what they need. See, there's power in your story."

Janay thought about what her mother said. Something about it rang true for her. Her marriage was a different issue.

"But what about my marriage? I'm mad that Evan got involved with Faith and now I have to exert energy fighting for my marriage. I get ticked off every time my children cry to be with her. It bothers me that my own husband is more concerned about Faith and her boyfriend than he is about me. I see the way he looks at her. I know he's in love with her, but what I don't know is if he loves me anymore. I really messed up."

"It sounds like you have some forgiving to do."

"If you're talking about forgiving Evan, I don't think that's going to happen. I cannot believe he did this."

"Evan thought you left him. He tried to stay faithful to your marriage. He figured you weren't coming back because you were gone so long. He was looking to fill the void. It just happened to be Faith because she was close, but it could've been anyone."

"You sound like you're taking his side."

"I'm just trying to get you to look at things from a different perspective. By the way, Evan isn't the only person you need to forgive."

"Faith?"

"Her, too. But, I was really talking about you. You feel guilty because you wanted some down time. There's nothing wrong with that. You just didn't communicate it well and led Evan to believe you didn't want the marriage anymore. It was a mistake. Let yourself off the hook."

"I know it was a mistake but mistakes sometimes carry consequences, too. I don't think it's fair to expect him to just turn his feelings off toward Faith. He wants her and I don't believe his heart is in repairing our relationship. I've spent a lot of time thinking about this. I've decided to let Evan go and just focus on my recovery and the girls."

"You'd better be sure that's really what you want to do. He might not be willing to entertain getting back together again. Think about that, daughter of mine."

"I don't know what else to do. How do I recover?"

"You're going to have to decide how much you want your marriage. Fight for it like you fought to make it out of that man's house. It took a strong person to make it through that. It's going to take a strong person to get through this. But, I believe it's worth it...if you want it," Big Momma advised.

Chapter 42

Janay fidgeted while she waited for Evan to finish showering. She fought the urge to place snacks and beverages out, but decided there would be no croissants and coffee in the family room this time. Only her, Evan and the truth. Still, she couldn't help feeling like this was deja vu. She wished she had never communicated her desire for a "leave of absence" from her family, considering what happened as a result. But, it was past time to address the pink and purple polka dot elephant, her and Evan's marriage. Someone had to initiate the discussion and apparently it wouldn't be Evan. So, she decided she would do it. Thankfully, her sister Cherlynn had taken the girls for a few hours to give Evan and Janay some privacy.

She heard Evan coming down the stairs and smoothed her denim wrap dress. The one he loved; at least he did before her kidnapping. He'd been acting so differently since she returned. He walked into the family room where she stood waiting for him to acknowledge her presence.

"Hi," she said shifting her weight from one foot to the other. *When did we become so awkward?*

"Hey," he said.

"Come. Sit down. Let's talk," Janay said as she sat on one end of the couch.

"Okay."

"How did we get here?" She asked, summarizing her concerns.

"There's no simple answer to that question."

"I know there's a lot to say, but I need to know about you and Faith. What is going on?" Janay unfolded her arms, trying to keep her body language welcoming. She didn't want to make Evan defensive because she needed some answers. Continuing her conversation, she said," When I talked to her, she was territorial and acted like I was the other woman. I don't quite understand that. Can you help me understand?"

"I'm not surprised she feels that way. Faith became a wife and mother while you were gone. Remember, I thought you abandoned us."

"A wife, huh?"

"She became my emotional support. There is nothing sexual about our relationship."

"Are you in love with her?"

"Wow, you're getting right into it aren't you?"

"Yes, because you haven't shown any sign of wanting to discuss it. So, are you?"

Evan subtly nodded his head. "I'm sorry, Janay. But if you're asking me to be honest...yes, I think I am."

"I never imagined I would be asking this of my own husband, but what does that mean for us?"

"While you were gone, I tried not to allow myself to think about you coming back. I couldn't bear expecting you and you not show up. It was easier to accept your absence. That way, I'd only have to heal once."

"Because of her?"

"No, because of me. I was devastated and I was trying to hold it together for the girls. Trying to figure out how to make it from one day to the next."

"You gave up on me?"

"No, I thought you gave up on us."

"I still don't know what that means for us."

"I don't know how to say this," he said making direct eye contact for the first time since he sat down.

"Just say it!" She yelled, forgetting all about being welcoming.

"I'm not sure I want to stay married to you, Janay. I think I've moved on."

Tears streamed down her cheeks as Evan confirmed her suspicion. She felt relief, then indignation and finally rage.

"Well, you can't move on. You don't have the right."

"Yes, I can and I think I have."

"You've been walking around here treating me like I'm some stranger; like I did you wrong. You won't even lay in bed with me. I didn't run off and leave you. You don't know all I went through in that basement. I went to the abyss and back while you were here with Faith hoping I wouldn't return and mess up your little arrangement. Well, I made it out. And now, after all I went through, you look me in the face and tell me you moved on? You, Evan Ingram, are not allowed." She stomped out of the room and headed to the master bedroom where she'd slept alone since her return. She slammed the door so hard she heard china rocking downstairs in the china cabinet. She hoped Evan heard it, too. *I didn't even get to tell him I still love him.*

***

Evan heard his wife slam the bedroom door. How had the conversation taken such a turn? She pressed for the truth like she already knew what he would say. Then, she became angry when she heard it. Evan hadn't wanted to have the discussion because of his feelings for Faith. However, Janay pushed until he acquiesced and committed to the discussion. He agreed it was time to settle things so everyone could get on with their respective lives.

After waiting for Janay to cool down a little, he decided to go upstairs and resolve the issue once and for all. There was no need to continue on like this. If they were going to end their marriage, the process needed to get started.

He tapped on the door and entered at the same time. Janay was sitting in a chair in the room looking out of the window, drying wetness from her face. Evan moved across the room and sat in the chair across from her. A small table separated them. Janay kept her gaze focused outside the window. Her brows met in the center of her forehead, the only acknowledgment of Evan's presence.

"I think we need to finish our conversation," Evan softly spoke.

"You're right," she responded wiping her face once again.

They spent a few moments in silence while Evan thought about what he should say next. Janay still hadn't looked at him so he knew he needed to consider her emotional state as well.

"All I wanted was some time for myself and now you're in love with somebody else. This is unbelievable."

"It doesn't mean I don't love you."

"I wish you loved me enough to let your infatuation with Faith go," Janay said, giving her husband eye contact.

Evan thought for a few moments and concluded Janay might have a point. He looked into his wife's eyes and saw his high school sweetheart, his best friend and lover. He saw the woman who gave birth to his daughters. He saw her as the strong woman she had to be to endure what she recently went through. He knew what he had to do.

"Baby, I'll be back."

Evan kissed her on her forehead and left the room. He was clear on his destination but not sure what would happen once he got there.

Chapter 43

Faith sat at her kitchen table feverishly searching online for a job. Since she hadn't heard from the Ingrams in weeks, she had to assume they were no longer interested in employing her. Though she didn't live extravagantly and Jamison took care of the house note, life still required money and that meant she needed to work.

She thought back on the time she spent with the Ingram family. They had become her family. Faith knew it was possible Janay would return, but each day that went by without her reappearing gave her hope the woman simply didn't want her family anymore. She assumed Janay wanted to recapture her youth and live out her life in a manner she couldn't with the responsibility of three young children and a husband. However, circumstances occurred leaving Faith without a job or a relationship with the family she adored.

Faith missed the Ns. She had been part of their upbringing since they were born. How was she going to adjust to not seeing their faces, hearing their voices and caring for them the way she had over the years? She missed Nahla's sensitivity, Nia's playful demeanor and Naomi's emerging personality.

If she was honest with herself, she missed Evan just as much. He found his way into a place in her heart she didn't expect. She knew it was a risk to allow him entrance considering he was a married man. The fact was it happened and since she was an adult, she needed to figure out how to adjust to the absence of all the Ingrams from her life. After all, she still had many years yet to live and she needed to fill them with as much love, joy and fun as possible.

The phone rang drawing Faith from her thoughts. She checked her caller id and saw Evan's phone number. It was just like the devil to cause this man to call her just when she'd resolved to release the possibility of a relationship with him. The phone continued to ring as she pondered whether to answer.

"Hello," Faith finally answered.

"Hi, um, this is Evan," he quietly responded.

"Yes, I know," she snapped.

"I know you're probably still upset with me. I apologize about what happened the last time we spoke. Will you forgive me?"

"I already have, but I'm not going to be treated that way again."

"It won't happen again," Evan mumbled.

"Are you whispering? I can barely hear you."

It sounded as though he was adjusting things so she could hear him better. "Is that better?"

"Not really. Is everything okay? You sound strange."

"No, things are a little tense, but we'll get through it."

"I see."

"I really miss you, Faith," Evan whispered.

"Wait a minute. Are you sneaking and calling me?"

"Do you expect me to boldly call you in front of Janay?"

"Well, if you've got to sneak, I would rather you not call me at all."

After a moment, Evan asked, "Is that really how you feel?"

Faith took a moment to think about her answer. "I can't continue to be in flux, waiting to see what happens. I need to close this chapter and start on the next one."

"I thought you said you wouldn't give up on us."

"Since you and Janay are working on your marriage, I think it's best I move on for my own well-being."

"Does that involve Jamison?" Evan asked.

"I'm not going to lie to you. Jamison and I are reconnecting and it's going well."

"I need to see you again."

"The last time you were here you insulted me, accusing me of taking advantage of you."

"If you let me come by, I promise it won't happen again. Please. I need to see you," Evan begged.

His pleading touched Faith in a way that had her considering taking a chance on a visit. She wrestled with her thoughts and responded from her head not her heart, "Evan, I don't think it would be wise."

"Please, Faith. Just this once. You'll see. It'll be okay."

Faith could only hope it would be okay because resisting this man was one of the most difficult things for her to do.

***

The doorbell rang indicating Evan's arrival. Faith opened the door to find Macie instead.

"Hey, what you doing, girl?"

"Um, hey," Faith responded, praying Evan wouldn't show up while Macie was there.

Macie looked at her as though she grew an additional head. "Why are you so dry? Aren't you glad to see me?" She asked taking a seat in Faith's living room.

The doorbell rang again. Faith wished a trap door would appear beneath her to avoid what she knew was about to happen. She knew she couldn't ignore the doorbell, though that's exactly what she wanted to do.

Faith looked at Macie and warned, "I need you to remember you dropped in unannounced. I don't want to hear a word from you after I open this door."

She opened the door and allowed Evan to enter. His eyes said he was surprised to see Macie and questioned her presence.

"Well, hello," Macie eyes perused Evan's body. "I see my friend has been keeping secrets. I'm Macie and you are?" She moved across the room and reached for Evan's hand. He responded by shaking hers.

"I'm Evan. It's nice to meet you, Macie. Faith, is this a bad time?"

Macie looked between Evan and Faith as realization washed over her face. "Really, now? No, it's not a bad time. Come on in," Macie responded taking a seat on Faith's couch.

"Macie, can I speak to you for a moment? Privately?" She motioned for her friend to follow her to another room.

"I'm not moving from this spot. You'll just have to work around me," she said as she swung her dangling foot.

"I can come back another time. It was a pleasure meeting you, Macie. Faith, I'll call you later." Evan held her hand for a moment and rubbed his thumb over it. How Faith wished Macie had left.

Macie leapt from her seated position and dislodged her friend's hand from Evan's. "Yeah, yeah, it was really nice meeting you, too. Shouldn't you be somewhere tending to your wife?" She said as she led him toward the door.

Faith couldn't believe what just happened, though she shouldn't have been surprised. Evan and Macie were never supposed to be in the same space. Nothing good could come from it. She didn't want Evan to leave because she wasn't sure if or when she would see him again.

"You have to leave Macie," Faith punctuated each word for emphasis.

Macie peered at Faith, placing her hands on her small hips and sneered as she spoke. "Since you're going to try to play me like that, I have a question before I go." She turned toward Evan with the same attitude. "Evan, are you planning to divorce Janay? Because if you're not, you need to man up and let Faith go. Don't put her in a position where her life is on hold while you're living yours with your wife and family. Give her a chance to do the same with someone like, um, Jamison. You know she deserves it."

Faith wasn't sure whether to be mad at Macie or not. On one hand, she wished she wouldn't have showed up tonight. This was supposed to be her opportunity to spend a little time with Evan. On the other hand, she agreed with Macie wholeheartedly. But, Faith wished she had allowed her to say it for herself. Granted, she didn't have the strength to stand by that declaration yet, but Evan should have heard it from her.

She looked over at Evan who seemed frozen in time. His chest appeared still, his mouth gaped open, hands in his pocket and one of his feet was in front of the other as if in mid-step. If his eyes hadn't blinked, Faith would've questioned whether he was alive.

"It's okay, Macie. I can handle this. Please," Faith spoke as she nudged her toward the door. "I'll call you tomorrow."

"I don't feel right about leaving. Someone has to have a clear head, considering neither of you do."

"Don't worry. It'll be okay." Faith begged Macie to leave her and Evan alone.

Macie's glare traveled between Evan and her. "Look, I'm only leaving because you asked. But hit me on my cell if you need backup, and I'll come right back over here." Her attention turned toward Evan. "And trust me, you don't want me to come back. Do the right thing."

Once Macie closed the door behind herself, Evan seemed to thaw as he took a deep breath. The two fell into each other's arms and Faith relaxed.

They stood in silence for several minutes, swaying from side to side. Faith knew this was likely her last time experiencing Evan this way. He pulled away from her and held her at arm's length.

"I think I have to attempt to repair my marriage. I owe it to Janay, the girls, and myself. As much as I want to be with you, I would always wonder if things could've worked out."

"I respect that," Faith said, trying to catch an errant tear from falling.

"If it doesn't work out, I'm going to show up on your doorstep again."

"Oh, so I'm your backup plan?"

"That's not it and you know it."

They both chuckled to relieve the tension building in the room.

"I'm going to miss you and the Ns. I'm concerned about how they'll take all of this."

"A wise woman once told me children are more resilient than we think."

Faith nodded in agreement.

He pulled her close one more time. They touched foreheads and looked into each other's eyes. Tears were present on both faces. There were smiles as well because of the fun times they shared and the closeness they developed.

Evan stepped away and turned toward the door. He stepped through it and closed it behind him for the last time. Faith fell to the floor, crying for all the time invested in Evan and his children.

Her phone rang and she quickly located it.

"Evan?" Faith answered thinking Evan had changed his mind.

"I just saw him leave. I'm coming in. Open the door," Macie spoke.

Faith followed her instruction and waited for her friend to enter her home. Macie found her sitting on the floor with mascara and eyeliner smudged all over her face. Sitting on the floor next to her without uttering a word, she drew Faith into her arms. Faith cried and slobbered all over her and Macie comforted her as only a good friend could. No judgment. No questions. No "I told you so."

Five months later...

Faith sat in the floor with the four new children she cared for playing a board game. It took her a couple of months to find children to fill the spots her small in-home daycare allowed. She loved caring for children and was thankful she was able to interact with them on a daily basis. She also appreciated having her weekends and evenings free for her personal life. She'd missed that while she worked for the Ingrams.

A text message notification startled her. She picked up her phone to read the message. It was from Evan.

Please come to the door.

Faith hadn't heard from Evan since they officially ended their relationship.

She struggled to get to the door in a timely fashion. She opened it to find Evan Ingram on her doorstep. Faith knew that meant something didn't go right with him and Janay and he was returning to resurrect their relationship.

She assessed the man standing on her porch with his hands in his pockets and a hopeful look on his face. She smiled at him and he returned the favor. He looked great. His clothing hung a little large on him, indicating he may have lost some weight. She felt something like electricity flow through her heart just being in his presence. Something about him still did it for her.

There was a time she would have fallen into his arms and welcomed the opportunity to be with him and gladly accepted whatever attention he had to give her. After they ended things, for a while, she prayed he would return so her heart could stop hurting. But that was then.

She didn't know what happened in the Ingram marriage and she wasn't going to ask. She had gotten involved before and decided it wasn't something she wanted to repeat. She refused to provide refuge for Evan with his on-again-off-again marriage. She wanted stability and she believed she'd found it in Jamison. She looked at her ring finger and admired the sparkle of the engagement ring there. Faith slowly closed the door. Her time as a make-believe wife was over.

The Make-Believe Wives
Discussion Questions

1) Was Janay's approach to dealing with her burnout appropriate? What could she have done differently?

2) Do you think the kidnapping was Janay's punishment for wanting a break from her family? Does God punish us because of our poor decisions?

3) Did Evan allow Faith to become a bigger part of the family to soothe his loneliness?

4) Who was at fault for Evan and Faith's relationship? Evan? Faith? Both?

5) At what point did Evan and Faith cross the line?

6) Was it right for Evan to move on with his life even though he didn't know where Janay was?

7) Did Evan hear from God about whether to divorce Janay?

8) Was Vonne wrong for not getting her brother help earlier? Was it her responsibility?

9) Should Vonne have turned Frank in after she discovered the kidnapping? Why or why not?

Dear Reader,

Thank you so much for reading *The Make-Believe Wives*. I hope you enjoyed it. My desire is that you take away a message that will have a positive impact on your life. If I achieve that goal, I did my job. I know there are millions of other books you could spend your time reading. I am honored you chose to read one of mine.

If you liked *The Make-Believe Wives*, please consider writing a review on the online retailer website of your choice. Also, visit me at my website, www.DarlissBatchelor.com. There, you'll learn about my other books, read excerpts, see video and much more. You will also have the opportunity to sign up for updates, giving you access to exclusive content, early release information, discounts and freebies.

Until the next book,

Darliss Batchelor

P.S. You can also find me on the web:
Website: www.DarlissBatchelor.com
Facebook: www.FaceBook.com/BooksByDarliss
Amazon Author Page: www.amazon.com/author/DarlissBatchelor
Goodreads: www.Goodreads.com/DarlissBatchelor

Other books by Darliss Batchelor

Secrets
Hell is a Skyscraper: A Trio of Novelettes
Something Else to Want

Available at
www.DarlissBatchelor.com

CPSIA information can be obtained
at www.ICGtesting.com
Printed in the USA
LVHW041948010120
642208LV00002B/182/P